Ally Carter

UNCOMMON CRIMINALS

Also by Ally Carter

Gallagher Girls series

Heist Society series

Embassy Row series

Ally Carter

UNCOMMON CRIMINALS

ORCHARD

ORCHARD BOOKS
First published in The United States in 2012
by Hyperion Books for Children
This edition published in 2018 by The Watts Publishing Group

1 3 5 7 9 10 8 6 4 2

A CIP catalogue record for this book is available from the British Library.

ISBN 978 1 40835 003 4

Printed and Bound by CPI Group (UK) Ltd, Croydon, CR0 4YY

The paper and board used in this book are made from wood
from responsible sources.

Orchard Books
An imprint of Hachette Children's Group
Part of The Watts Publishing Group Limited
Carmelite House
50 Victoria Embankment
London EC4Y 0DZ
An Hachette UK Company
www.hachette.co.uk

www.hachettechildrens.co.uk

For Vanessa

ONE

Moscow can be a cold, hard place in winter. But the big old house on Tverskoy Boulevard had always seemed immune to these particular facts, the way that it had seemed immune to many things throughout the years.

When breadlines filled the streets during the reign of the czars, the big house had caviar. When the rest of Russia stood shaking in the Siberian winds, that house had fires and gaslight in every room. And when the Second World War was over and places like Leningrad and Berlin were nothing but rubble and crumbling walls, the residents of the big house on Tverskoy Boulevard only had to take up a hammer and drive a single nail – to hang a painting on the landing at the top of the stairs – to mark the end of a long war.

The canvas was small, perhaps only eight by ten inches. The brushstrokes were light but meticulous. And the subject, the countryside near Provence, was once a favourite of an artist named Cézanne.

No one in the house spoke of how the painting had come to be there. Not a single member of the staff ever asked the man of the house, a high-ranking Soviet official, to talk about the canvas or the war or whatever services he may have performed in battle or beyond to earn such a lavish prize. The house on Tverskoy Boulevard was not one for stories, everybody knew. And besides, the war was over. The Nazis had lost. And to the victors went the spoils.

Or, as the case may be, the paintings.

Eventually, the wallpaper faded, and soon few people actually remembered the man who had brought the painting home from the newly liberated East Germany. None of the neighbours dared to whisper the letters K-G-B. Of the old Socialists and new socialites who flooded through the open doors for parties, not one ever dared to mention the Russian mob.

And still the painting stayed hanging, the music kept playing, and the party itself seemed to last – echoing out onto the street, fading into the frigid air of the night.

The party on the first Friday of February was a fundraiser – though for what cause or foundation, no one really knew. It didn't matter. The same people were invited. The same chef was preparing the same food. The men stood smoking the same cigars and drinking the same vodka. And, of course, the same painting still hung at the top of the stairs, looking down on the partygoers below.

But one of the partygoers was not, actually, the same.

When she gave the man at the door a name from the list, her Russian bore a slight accent. When she handed her coat to a maid, no one seemed to notice that it was far too light for someone who had spent too long in Moscow's winter. She was too short; her black hair framed a face that was in every way too young. The women watched her pass, eyeing the competition. The men hardly noticed her at all as she nibbled and sipped and waited until the hour grew late and the people became tipsy. When that time finally came, not one soul watched as the girl with the soft pale skin climbed the stairs and slipped the small painting from the nail that held it. She walked to the window.

And jumped.

And neither the house on Tverskoy Boulevard nor any of its occupants ever saw the girl or the painting again.

TWO

No one visits Moscow in February just for fun.

Perhaps that is why the customs agent looked so curiously at the shorter-than-average teenage girl who stood in line behind the business people and expatriates who were arriving in New York that day, choosing to flee the Russian winter.

"How long was your visit?" the agent asked.

"Three days," was the girl's reply.

"Do you have anything to declare?" The customs agent lowered her head, studied the girl from over the top of her half-moon glasses. "Are you bringing anything home with you, sweetie?"

The girl seemed to consider this, then shook her head. "No."

When the woman asked, "Are you travelling by yourself?" she sounded less like a government official doing her due diligence and more like a mother concerned that such a young girl could be travelling the world alone.

But the girl seemed perfectly at ease as she smiled and said, "Yes."

"And were you travelling for business or for pleasure?" the

woman asked, looking from the pale blue customs form to the girl's bright blue eyes.

"Pleasure," the young girl said. She reached for her passport. "I had to go to a party."

Even though she'd just landed in New York, when Katarina Bishop walked through the airport that Saturday afternoon, her mind couldn't help but drift to all the places she still had to go.

There was a Klimt in Cairo, a very nice Rembrandt rumoured to be hidden in a cave in the Swiss Alps, and a statue by Bartolini last seen somewhere on the outskirts of Buenos Aires. Altogether, there were at least a half dozen jobs that could come next, and Kat's thoughts wandered through them like a maze. And still the part that weighed heaviest on her were the jobs she didn't know about – the plundered treasures no one had found yet. The Nazis had needed an army, she told herself, to steal them all. But she was just one girl – one thief. She felt exhausted, remembering it might take a lifetime to steal them all back.

When she stepped onto the long escalator and began her descent, Kat was completely unaware of the tall boy with the broad shoulders behind her until she felt the weight of her bag rise gently off her shoulder. She turned and looked up, but didn't smile.

"You'd better not be trying to steal that," she said.

The boy shrugged and reached for the small rolling suitcase at her feet. "I wouldn't dare."

"Because I'm an excellent yeller."

"I don't doubt it."

"And fighter. My cousin gave me this nail file...the thing's just like a switchblade."

The boy nodded slowly. "I'll keep that in mind."

When they reached the bottom of the escalator, Kat stepped onto the smooth floor and realised how insane – and incredibly sloppy – it was for her not to have seen the boy that every other woman in the terminal was openly staring at. It wasn't because he was handsome (though he was); it wasn't because he was wealthy (though that too was undeniable); there was simply something about W. W. Hale the Fifth – a confidence that Kat knew could not be bought (and almost certainly could never be stolen).

So she let him carry her bags. She didn't protest when he walked so close that her shoulder brushed against the arm of his heavy wool coat. And yet, beyond that, they did not touch. He didn't even look at her as he said, "I would have sent the jet."

"See –" she glanced up at him – "I'm trying to build up the miles."

"Oh, well, when you put it that way..." A split second later, Kat saw her passport appear in Hale's hands as if by magic. "So, how was Moscow, Ms...McMurray." He eyed her. "You don't look like a Sue."

"Moscow was cold," Kat answered.

He flipped the page of the passport and examined the stamps. "And Rio?"

"Hot."

"And—"

"I thought my dad and Uncle Eddie summoned you to Uruguay?" She stopped suddenly.

"Paraguay," he corrected. "And it was more *invitation* than summons. I regretfully declined. Besides, I really wanted to do a Smash and Grab job in a mansion with half the former KGB." He gave a long sigh. "Too bad I never got that invitation."

Kat looked at him. "It was more like a *Gab* and Grab."

"That's too bad." Hale smiled, but Kat felt very little warmth in the gesture. "You know, I've been told that I can really wear a tuxedo."

Kat did know. She'd actually been there when her cousin Gabrielle had told him. But tuxedos, Kat knew, weren't really the issue.

"It was an easy job, Hale." Kat remembered the cold wind in her hair as she'd stood in the open window. She thought about the empty nail that had probably gone unnoticed until morning, and she had to laugh. "Totally easy. You would have been bored."

"Yeah," he said. "Because *easy* and *boring* are two words I frequently associate with the KGB."

"I was fine, Hale." She reached for him. "I'm serious. It was a one-person job. If I'd needed help I would have called, but—"

"I guess you just didn't need the help."

"The family is in Uruguay."

"Paraguay," he corrected.

"The family is in *Paraguay*," Kat said louder, but then she felt herself go quiet. "I thought you were with the family."

He stepped towards her, reached out, and slid the passport into her jacket pocket, just above her heart. "I'd hate to see you lose this."

When he started outside, Kat watched the big glass doors slide open. She braced herself against the freezing wind, but Hale seemed immune to the cold as he turned and called behind him, "So – a Cézanne, huh?"

She held two fingers inches apart. "Just a little one... Weatherby?" she guessed, but Hale merely laughed as a long black car pulled to the kerb. "Wendell?" Kat guessed again, hurrying to catch up. She slid between the boy and the car, and standing there, with his face inches from hers, the truth about what the *W*'s in his name stood for didn't seem to matter at all. The reasons she'd been working all winter were blowing away with the breeze.

Hale's *here*.

But then he inched closer – to her and to a line that couldn't be uncrossed – and Kat felt her heart change rhythms.

"Excuse me," a deep voice said. "Miss, excuse me."

It took a moment for Kat to actually hear the words, to step back far enough to allow the man to reach for the door. He had grey hair, grey eyes, and a grey wool overcoat, and the effect, Kat thought, was that he was part butler, part driver, and part literal man of steel.

"You missed me, didn't you, Marcus?" she asked as he

took her bags and carried them to the open boot with a graceful ease.

"Indeed," he said in a thick British accent, the origin of which Kat had long ago stopped trying to pinpoint. Then, with a tip of his hat, he finished, "Welcome home, miss."

"Yeah, Kat," Hale said slowly. "Welcome home."

The car, no doubt, was warm. The roads to Uncle Eddie's brownstone or Hale's country house were all free from snow and ice, and the two of them might have been settled someplace dry and safe within the hour.

But Marcus's hand lingered on the door handle a second too long. Kat's fifteen years as Uncle Eddie's great-niece and Bobby Bishop's daughter had left her senses a bit too sharp. And the wind was blowing in just the right direction, perfectly calibrated to carry the word on the air as a voice screamed, "Katarina!"

In all of Kat's life, only three people routinely called her by her full first name. One had a voice that was deep and gruff, and he was currently giving orders in Paraguay. Or Uruguay. One had a voice that was soft and kind and he was in Warsaw, examining a long-lost Cézanne, preparing plans to take it home. But it was the last voice that Kat feared as she spun away from the car, because the last voice, let's face it, belonged to the man who most likely wanted to kill her.

Kat stared down the long line of taxis picking up fares, travellers hugging and saying hello. She waited. She watched. But none of those three people came into view.

"Katarina?"

There was a woman walking towards her. She had white hair and kind eyes and wore a long tweed coat and a hand-knitted scarf wrapped around her neck. The young man at her side kept his arm around the woman's shoulders, and the two of them moved slowly – as if Kat were made out of smoke and she might float away on the breeze.

"Are you *the* Katarina Bishop?" the woman asked, eyes wide. "Are you the girl who robbed the Henley?"

THREE

If a person wanted to be technical about it, Katarina Bishop did not rob the Henley – nor did any member of her crew. She was simply one of a group of teenagers who had walked into the most secure museum in the world a few months before and removed from its walls four paintings that were not the Henley's property. The paintings appeared on no insurance statements. They were never listed in any catalogues. The Henley had never paid a dime for any of those works, so even as Kat herself carried one (a Rembrandt) out of the museum's doors, she was not breaking a single law. (A technicality verified by Uncle Marco – a member of the family who had once spent eighteen months impersonating a federal judge somewhere in Minnesota.)

So it was with absolutely no hesitation that Kat looked at the woman and said, "I'm sorry. You've been misinformed."

"*You're* Katarina Bishop?" the woman's companion asked, and although Kat had never met him before, it was a question and a tone she had heard a lot since last December.

The girl who'd planned the job at the Henley should have

been taller, the question seemed to say. She should have been older, wiser, stronger, faster, and just in general *more* than the short girl who stood before them.

"*The* Katarina Bishop..." The man paused, searching for words, then whispered, "The thief?"

That, as it turned out, was not an easy question to answer. After all, stealing – even for noble and worthy causes – was illegal. Furthermore, if their accents were to be believed, they were *English* strangers, and England was home to the Henley, the Henley's trustees, and, perhaps most important, the Henley's insurance company.

But the primary reason Kat couldn't – or didn't – answer was that she no longer considered herself a thief. Kat was more of a return artist, a repossession specialist. A highly uncommon criminal. After all, the statue she'd swiped in Rio rightfully belonged to a woman whose grandparents had died in Auschwitz. The painting from Moscow would soon be winging its way towards a ninety-year-old man in Tel Aviv.

So no, Katarina Bishop was not a thief, and that was why she said, "I'm afraid you have the wrong person," and turned back to Hale and the long black limousine.

"We need your help." The woman moved towards her.

"I'm sorry," Kat said.

"We were led to believe that you were quite talented."

"Talent is overrated," was Kat's reply.

She stepped closer to the car, but the woman reached for her arm. "We can pay!"

At this, Kat had to stop.

"I'm afraid you *really* have the wrong person."

With one look from Kat, Hale reached for the limo door. Kat was halfway inside when the woman called, "He said you...help people." Her voice cracked, and the young man tightened his grip around her shoulders.

"Grandmother, let's go. We shouldn't have believed him."

"Who?" The word was sharper than she'd intended, but Kat couldn't help herself. She climbed from the car. "Who told you my name? Someone said where you could find me, who was it?"

"A man..." the woman muttered, fumbling for words. "He was very convincing. He said—"

"What was his name?" Hale stepped closer to the young man, who had maybe eight years and two inches on him.

"He came to our flat..." the man started, but the woman's whisper was all that Kat could hear.

"Romani." She drew a deep breath. "He said his name was Visily Romani."

FOUR

Perhaps you have never heard the name Visily Romani. Until two separate cards bearing that name appeared at the Henley four months before, very few people ever had. Kat had never heard those words until that time, but Kat was still a very young person in a very old world. Since then, Kat herself would say, she'd got much, much older.

At least that was how she felt an hour later as she sat beside Hale in a small quiet diner not far from Uncle Eddie's brownstone on the Brooklyn side of the bridge. The old woman and her companion sat on the other side of the booth. Wordless and worn, both looking as if they'd travelled a long, long way to get there.

The place was nearly empty, and yet the young man kept looking over his shoulder at the waitress wiping down tables and the college girl who sat by the window wearing headphones and studying a book on constitutional law. He took the room in with sharp brown eyes behind horn-rimmed glasses.

When he asked, "Are you sure we shouldn't go someplace more private?" he actually sounded afraid.

"This is private enough," Hale answered.

"But—" the guy started, but then Kat placed her elbows on the table.

"Who are you and why are you looking for me?"

"My name is Constance Miller, Miss Bishop," the white-haired woman said. "Or, may I call you by your given name? I feel as if I know you – you and Mr Hale." She smiled at Hale. "Such a lovely young couple." Kat shifted on her seat, but the old woman went on. "I've become something of a fan." She sounded almost giddy, as if her whole life had been comprised of bake sales and Agatha Christie novels, and now she found herself inside the latter.

"I mean to say," the woman went on, "that there's something I would like for you to steal."

"Grandmother, *please*."

"Oh, Marshall," the woman said, patting her grandson's hands, "*they're professionals*."

Hale raised his eyebrows and smirked at Kat. Kat kicked him and gestured for the woman to go on.

"But, Grandmother, they're..." He glanced across the table and dropped his voice. "Kids."

"You're twenty-five," she told him.

"What does that have to do with anything?"

She shrugged. "To me, you're all children."

Kat didn't want to like this woman. Affection makes people get sloppy, take risks. Do favours. So Kat didn't allow herself to smile. She just focused on the single thing she really had to know.

"How did you meet Visily Romani?"

"He came to see me in London two weeks ago. He was familiar with our situation and said that you—"

"What did he look like?" Kat found herself leaning across the table, pushing closer to the only person she'd ever met who'd looked Romani in the eye. "What did he say? Did he give you anything or—"

"Have you ever been to Egypt, Katarina?" the old woman asked, but didn't wait for a reply. "I was born there." She smiled then. "Oh, it was a beautiful place to be a child. The cities were alive and the deserts were so big and vast – like the ocean, you see. We slept under big white nets and played in the sun. My father, he was a brilliant man. Strong and brave and gutsy," the woman said with a shake of a fist. "He was an archaeologist – he *and* my mother – and in that day...well...in that day, Egypt was the only place to be."

"That's nice, ma'am, but I believe you said something about—" Hale started, but the woman kept on going.

"Some looked at the sand and the sun and said it was a barren, uncivilised land. But my father and mother, they knew that it is not the surface of a place that matters. Civilisation is not made out of sand – it's made out of blood. My parents searched for years. Wars raged, and they searched. Children were born, and they searched. The past, it called to them." Her gaze shifted into space. "As I guess now it calls to me."

Kat nodded and thought of the treasures stolen more than a half-century before, paintings she had never seen that she longed to touch and hold.

"Grandmother," Marshall said softly, laying a hand on the woman's shoulder, "perhaps we should get you some tea."

"I don't want tea! I want justice!" Her frail fist banged the table. "I want that man to lose his stone just like my parents lost everything they had!"

"Stone?" Hale said, sitting straighter. "What stone?"

But the guy didn't even acknowledge the question. "Come, Grandmother, if the best lawyers in England can't help us, what are two kids—"

"Kids who robbed the Henley," Hale added. Kat kicked him under the table again.

"—supposed to do about it?" Marshall finished.

"My parents found it, Katarina." Suddenly, the woman's hands were reaching out to hold Kat's thin fingers in her own. "They found it – a hundred kilometres from Alexandria, just a stone's throw from the sea. They found it – one of the treasure chambers of the last pharaoh in Egypt."

"The last pharaoh..." Kat started.

The woman sighed and whispered, "I suppose you might know her better as Cleopatra."

When Kat's fingers began to tingle, she didn't know if it was the woman's words or her grasp that numbed her.

"Oh, it was a glorious sight. Cleopatra had known her empire's days were numbered, and she'd taken great care to hide her finest treasures from the Romans. The chamber was the largest my parents had ever seen. Urns and statues and gold...so much gold. I remember playing hide-and-seek with the diggers in mountains of gold so high, they might as well have been made of sand."

She unclasped the purse that sat on her lap and drew a faded black-and-white photograph from the inner lining. Her hands seemed especially frail as she held it, staring down at a memory.

"That was the happiest I'd ever been," the woman said, holding the photo out to Kat and Hale like an offering. Kat leaned across the cheap diner table and studied the image of a young girl in a white dress standing among the treasures of a queen.

"What happened?" Hale said again.

"Kelly...happened," the grandson spoke, and the sound of that name was all it took to wipe the smile from the woman's face.

"I never liked him, and you should always trust the instincts of children," she said, then laughed softly. "But I suppose you already know that."

Kat nodded and said, "Go on."

"Well, my parents found the chamber, and three days into the documentation process, my mother went into premature labour with my brother. It was terrible. We almost lost both of them. But my parents had discovered the find of their careers, so they were happy. My father had a young assistant whom he left to oversee the work while my mother recovered. Two weeks, my parents were gone. *Two weeks.*" The last words she said no louder than a whisper. "Do you know how much your life can change in two weeks?"

Kat felt Hale's leg pressing against hers under the table, but neither of them said a word. Neither of them had to.

"He took it all, Miss Bishop. In the two weeks my mother lay near death, my parents' assistant took everything they'd worked for their entire lives."

"He claimed the find?" Kat guessed.

"Worse," the woman said. "He packed everything up and began to sell it. Not one piece was logged. Nothing was chronicled or examined. Artefacts were crammed into steamers and hauled across the Mediterranean. History was sold to the highest bidder at a time when the world paid very well for the treasures of the kings. Or queens, as the case may be."

Then the woman reached for a handkerchief, but she didn't start to cry. She just studied Kat and Hale and told them, "My parents were discredited and penniless – the laughing stock of the archaeological world. The find of their careers was gone – taken by the person they'd trusted most."

"But surely they'd told people?" Hale didn't even try to hide the scepticism in his voice. "Surely someone knew what they'd been working on and what they'd found."

"Oh, but it was a wild place, Mr Hale. Those were dangerous times. Looters were everywhere – grave robbers, treasure seekers. Real archaeologists were incredibly careful with their work. Secrecy was paramount."

"But after..." Kat started.

The woman huffed. "After? After, they were broken and abandoned. After, they had nothing but their pride and their children. I, Miss Bishop... My brother and I were the only things they carried out of that sand, and soon I too will turn to dust." She took a deep breath, and her delicate hands gripped the handkerchief tighter. "It is too late for my parents to have what was theirs. But it's not too late for Egypt to have what is Egypt's."

She placed her palms on the table and leaned forward, a new urgency in her eyes. It was the look of a woman with a purpose – a plan.

"There is a museum in Cairo that will take the stone if I can deliver it to them. They should have had it a half-century ago, but better late than never." Then she stopped. She seemed to be studying Kat anew when she said, "It must be a wonderful feeling to take something beautiful and return it to its rightful home. Wouldn't you agree, Katarina?"

"What..." Kat shook her head. "What did Visily Romani tell you about me?"

"That you steal things." Again, the woman gave a soft laugh. Kat tried to see something of the girl from the picture in her eyes, but too much time and sun and sand stood between them.

Hale sat up a little straighter. "Your parents' assistant's name was Kelly?"

The woman smiled. "Yes."

"Oliver Kelly?" Hale asked.

The woman laughed again and searched Kat's eyes. "Yes, Katarina, the founder of the world's greatest auction house was a coward, a plunderer...a *thief*."

Outside, a cold rain was falling. Kat could hear the drops landing against the diner's windows, and she thought of Warsaw and the look in Abiram Stein's eyes as he'd talked about war and Nazis and paintings.

"Look at that picture, Katarina." The woman slid the snapshot further across the table.

"It's a lovely—"

"*Look closer.*"

Kelly. Egypt. Cleopatra. The words filled the room like the aroma of coffee and sound of the rain. Kat looked down once more and saw a little girl in a long white dress, an ornate room, two tanned hands, and the largest gem that Katarina Bishop had ever seen.

"Is that—"

"Yes."

"So this is—"

The grandson swallowed. "Yes."

"And you want us to—"

"Your friend Mr Romani assured us that you're perfectly qualified. If it's a matter of financing, I'm afraid our legal efforts have left us rather poorer than we once were, but we have some assets we could liquidate. This –" the woman gripped an antique locket that hung from a chain around her neck – "I know a dealer who would give me five hundred pounds for it."

"It's not money," Kat said, shaking her head. "It's just that...you want us to track down and steal the Cleopatra Emerald?"

"*The* Cleopatra Emerald?" Hale added for emphasis.

"Oh yeah." For the first time, the grandson smiled. "The one that's cursed."

FIVE

It didn't matter that it was raining when Kat and Hale left the diner – they waved Marcus and the long black car away. It felt good, somehow, to walk in the cold wind with their collars turned up, shivering against the dreary mist. Their thoughts, after all, were on Egypt and sand.

And curses.

"They were nice." Hale kept his hands in his pockets but raised his face to the sky, water pebbling on his skin.

"Yes" was Kat's reply.

"Nice is...refreshing."

Kat laughed and turned automatically onto a narrow street. "Yeah."

"And risky."

"Uh-huh."

"And they seem like the sort of people who could really use help."

"From someone good," Kat offered.

"From someone stupid." Hale stopped so suddenly that Kat walked past him. She had to turn to see him say,

"But we're not stupid, are we, Kat?"

"No. Of course—"

"So under no circumstances are we going to take this job?"

"Of course not," Kat said, just as the rain turned to sheets, hard and cold. Hale gripped her hand and pulled her onto a familiar stoop, under the shallow overhang of the roof above. She shivered, the wooden door at her back, while Hale leaned close, sheltering her, searching her eyes.

The windows of the brownstone were black, and the street was empty. There were no cars, no nannies pushing strollers or pedestrians jogging home. It felt to Kat as if she and Hale were the only two people in New York City. They could steal anything they wanted.

But I don't steal any more, Kat told herself. *Don't steal anything at all.*

"No one's home," she told him.

Water clung to the corners of his mouth. "We could pick a lock. Jimmy open a window."

"You know, I bet there's a hide-a-key around here somewhere," she tried to tease, but Hale had moved even closer. She couldn't see the street. She couldn't feel the rain. Her passport was in her pocket, and when he pressed against her, she could almost feel the stamps burning, telling the world that she'd been away from home a long time.

Hale's hands were on her neck – warm and big and comforting. Strange and new and different.

Kat feared she hadn't been gone long enough.

"Kat," Hale whispered. His breath felt warm against her

skin. "When you take this job, don't even think about stealing that emerald without me."

Kat tried to pull away, but the door was there, pressing against her back. "I'm not going to—"

But then she couldn't finish because *nothing* was against her back. Kat found herself falling, reaching for Hale, but her hands grasped only air until she was flat on her back in the doorway.

"Hello, Kitty Kat." Kat stared up at a familiar pair of long legs and a short skirt. Her cousin Gabrielle crossed her arms and stared down. "Welcome home."

Kat hadn't realised how cold she was until she found herself lying on the floor of the old brownstone. There was no fire in the fireplace, no lights in the parlour or on the stairs. For a second, it felt almost like a job, as if she shouldn't be there. And maybe, she realised, she shouldn't be.

"We didn't know anyone was home," Kat said.

Gabrielle laughed. "I could tell."

Even in the darkness, Kat could see a glimmer in her cousin's eyes. A glimmer of what, however, she didn't dare to ask. She just watched Gabrielle turn and saunter down the long hall, moving through the shadows, weightless as a ghost.

When Kat climbed to her feet and followed, Hale at her back, she heard the squeaky floorboards, the moaning of the old house in the storm. It seemed too big. Too dark. Too empty.

"Wow. He really left," Hale said, dismayed.

"Yeah." Gabrielle reached the doorway to the kitchen and exhaled a short quick laugh. "I don't think Uncle Bobby was too happy about it, either – no one thought Eddie would actually go all the way to Paraguay. But you've probably heard all about that." She studied her cousin through the dim light. "You *have* talked to your dad, haven't you?"

"Of course I have," Kat said, reaching for the light switch.

When the lights flickered to life, Kat had to squint against the glare. She half expected her uncle to mysteriously appear, spoon in hand, complaining that she was late and the soup was cold.

"How is Paraguay?" Hale asked, oblivious to the ghost that Kat was sensing, squeezing past her and into the kitchen as if he'd been at home there his whole life.

"OK, I guess," Gabrielle said with a shrug. "Or as OK as a job this big ever goes. All hands on deck." She sat down, threw her feet onto the table, and eyed her cousin. "Well... *almost* all hands." She pulled a knife from her boot and an apple from a bowl and began to peel it in one long steady spiral. "So, are you guys gonna tell me what the big secret is?" She glanced from Kat to Hale then back again. "Because it looked like you were getting fairly cosy out there, talking about something. Or maybe you *weren't* talking..."

Kat felt herself start to blush, but before she could say a thing, Hale opened the refrigerator and announced, "Kat's going to steal the Cleopatra Emerald."

"That's funny," Gabrielle said. It took a moment for her knife hand to pause in mid-air. "It is funny, isn't it?"

Kat's gaze was burning into Hale. "I never said I was going to do it," she told him. "I never said—"

"Of course you're going to do it." The refrigerator door slammed, and Hale turned. "I mean, it's what you do now, isn't it? Travel the world, righting wrongs. A one-woman recovery crew."

Kat wanted to reply, but Gabrielle's feet were already off the table, and she was leaning closer to Kat, knife in hand.

"Tell me he's joking, Kat... Tell me you are not seriously thinking about stealing the Cleopatra Emerald."

"No," Kat said. "I mean...well...we just met this woman who says the emerald was really discovered by her parents—"

"Constance Miller," Gabrielle filled in.

"You know her?" Kat said.

"I know everything there is to know about the most valuable emerald in the world, Kat. *I'm a thief.*"

"So am I," Kat shot back, but her cousin just talked on.

"I'm serious. The Cleopatra Emerald is ninety-seven karats of crazy!"

"I know."

Behind her, Kat heard Hale throwing open cabinet doors. "Where's the microwave?"

"Uncle Eddie doesn't *have* a microwave!" the cousins snapped in unison, but neither of them smiled. Neither girl joked. They kept staring at each other across the scarred wooden table that had seen the rise and fall of almost every major heist their family had ever done.

It seemed as fitting a place as any for Gabrielle to say,

"You don't want to do this, Kat. You do not want to forget that the Cleopatra Emerald is the most heavily guarded gem on the planet. It hasn't even seen the light of day in thirty years."

"I know," Kat told her.

"Anybody with any sense would know that Constance Miller is an old recluse who's almost out of money." Gabrielle looked her shorter, paler cousin up and down. "And she must be especially desperate if she's coming to you."

"Thanks," Kat said.

"And, most of all," Gabrielle went on, "we *real* thieves know that the Cleopatra Emerald has been cursed ever since Cleopatra took the biggest emerald in the world and, in all her wisdom, decided to split it down the middle and give half to Mark Antony. Then he went off to battle the Romans—"

"And died," Hale chimed in from behind them.

"Cleopatra kept the other half," Gabrielle went on.

"And died," Hale said again.

"And until the two stones are together again, they will bring nothing but death and destruction to whoever holds either one," Gabrielle finished. She stood and stepped closer to her cousin. "So any good thief would know it's cursed, Kat."

"There's no such thing as curses," Kat tried to retort, but the taller girl was already crossing her arms and looking down in a way that made Kat feel especially small.

"Then how do you explain what happened when Uncle Nester went after it in '79?"

"Lasers burn things, Gabrielle. It's not the emerald's fault Uncle Nester was sloppy with his fingers."

"And what about the Garner Brothers in 1981?"

"Hey, anyone who thinks a non-military–grade rappelling cable can support the weight of two grown men *and* a miniature donkey deserves to fall off a cliff."

"And that Japanese team in 2000?"

"You should always take a backup defibrillator if you're gonna try the Sleeping Beauty. Everybody knows that. Besides, Uncle Eddie didn't care when he went after it in '67," Kat tried.

Gabrielle's glare turned icy. "He cares now."

"What happened in '67?" Hale asked, but neither girl seemed to hear nor care.

Gabrielle eased forward, silent and deadly as a snake. "The most important thing I know, Kitty Kat, is that Uncle Eddie – arguably the world's greatest living thief – says that the Cleopatra Emerald is *not* to be stolen. I know that whatever happened in '67 was enough to scare *Uncle Eddie*, so I believe him when he says that Cleopatra jobs end badly. Kat, they always end badly." She dropped into her chair and crossed her long legs. "I don't know what sob story Constance Miller gave you, or how a woman who supposedly hasn't left her house in years managed to find you, or why–"

"Visily Romani," Kat heard herself whisper, and she watched Gabrielle's eyes go wide. "They knew the name Romani. They said Visily Romani sent them."

It was easy to forget that there were some things with more

history than Uncle Eddie's kitchen table, but at the sound of the ancient name, Gabrielle's hands went to the scarred wood, and two words filled Kat's mind: *Chelovek Pseudonima*.

Alias Man, Uncle Eddie had translated for her once, and so Kat sat there, thinking about the old names, the sacred names. Names used for hundreds of years, but only by the best thieves, and for only the most worthy causes. Kat trembled, knowing those causes now included the Cleopatra Emerald.

"He's still out there," Kat said. "This man who calls himself Romani – whoever he is – he's still out there, and he sent me these people because I can help them. He thinks I can do this. I can—"

"Not you, Kat. We." Hale dropped into a seat at the head of the table. He didn't look at her. "If *you* do this, then *we* do this."

"Of course. Yeah. *We*. But it's not like it matters anyway," Kat told them with a shake of her head. "The Cleopatra is supposed to be locked up somewhere in Switzerland. And even if we could find it...What? What are you staring at?"

Gabrielle looked at Hale, who shook his head, leaving Gabrielle to shuffle through the stack of mail that sat unopened on the end of the table.

"You've been gone, Kitty Kat." Gabrielle slid the newspaper across the table, the headline blaring out for all to see that the Kelly Corporation was finally going to bring its most prized possession home.

Home.

New York.

Kat felt her heart beat faster as she looked first at Gabrielle and then at Hale.

"So...what?" Hale asked slowly. "I guess now we steal an emerald?"

There was a room at the top of the stairs that had white eyelet curtains and two twin beds with matching quilts. There was a small dresser, a wicker hamper and a bookshelf full of dusty, fraying Nancy Drews. That room had never belonged with the rest of the house, Kat had always thought. Stepping inside was like walking into another world – one with a pink rotary telephone and a music box. A tiny alcove in a man's world, a place made entirely for girls.

Someone, sometime had embroidered the name *Nadia* on a pillow, and Kat held it in her arms as she lay, staring up at the ceiling but not sleeping. She felt too small, lying on her mother's bed, still trying to fit inside her footsteps.

"So, *Hale*..."

Kat turned and saw Gabrielle silhouetted in the door, watched her walk to the other bed and lie down atop a pillow with the willowy script that spelled the name *Irina*.

"What about him?"

"What's going on with you two?"

"Nothing," Kat said, a little too quickly.

"Yeah, and why is that exactly? I thought you two were getting all relationshipy. But now you're gone half of the time and he's...*angry*."

"No, he's not."

"Yes, he is." Gabrielle gave a short laugh. "He doesn't like you going off, doing these jobs on your own." Kat drew a breath to protest, but not before her cousin lowered her voice and added, "*And he's not the only one.*"

Kat honestly didn't know what to say, so she turned onto her side and closed her eyes. She didn't even know that Gabrielle had crossed the room until she felt her cousin's weight plop down on the mattress beside her. "So why are you doing it?"

"I..." Kat stumbled, looking for the words in the dark. "They're easy jobs, Gabrielle."

"Maybe in the beginning, but Rio wasn't easy."

"How do you know about Rio?"

"Everyone knows about Rio. Everyone would have helped."

Kat's throat was suddenly too dry. "I didn't need any help."

"And what about Moscow?" her cousin went on. "Maybe you didn't *need* help, but whenever you start going up against the KGB, you should probably get some – just in case. So the question is...why didn't you?" Gabrielle rested her elbows on her knees and tapped her chin, thinking.

"Gabrielle, I'm—"

"Drunk!" Gabrielle exclaimed, bolting upright with the realisation.

"I've never been drunk in my life," Kat shot back, but her cousin only laughed.

"Oh, you're heist-drunk, Kitty Kat. And you have been since the Henley."

Kat tried to push herself up and out of the bed, but Gabrielle was perched atop the covers, pinning her in.

"Tell me you didn't feel a rush when we carried those paintings out of the museum's front door... Tell me there wasn't a high when you swiped a Cézanne under the noses of half the KGB... No wonder you aren't taking Hale with you." She shook her head. "Sometimes boys are far easier to deal with when they're on the other side of the world."

"Hale and I aren't..." But Kat trailed off, completely unsure how that sentence was supposed to end. "You don't know what you're talking about, Gabrielle," she started again, but her cousin shook her head.

"Yeah. I do," Gabrielle said, insulted. "Our world is built on adrenaline and getting away with it. Different cities, different names. It's a far simpler life to lead when there's no one around to tell you when you're being stupid. Believe me, dear cousin –" Gabrielle stood and stretched – "I know better than anyone."

Kat had often wondered what really went on inside Gabrielle's totally beautiful head. More than met the eye, she was certain.

"Look, Gabrielle. These are my jobs – my call. There's nothing in it for anyone – no pay cheque – so there's no sense asking anyone else to take the risk. I'm not on some kind of bender here."

"Sure," Gabrielle said, nodding slowly. "And six months

ago, you went off to the Colgan School and swore you were never going to steal again." She crossed the room in two long strides. "You're off the wagon, Kitty Kat. And the least you can do is admit it."

Kat rolled over and stared at the ceiling again. It seemed to take forever to say, "Hale...how mad is he?"

Gabrielle crawled into bed and looked at her cousin across the shadowy space. "For a genius thief, you really are a stupid girl, aren't you?"

"Yeah." Kat closed her eyes. "I am."

4 DAYS BEFORE
THE EMERALD ARRIVES

BROOKLYN, NEW YORK
USA

SIX

"My name is Ezra Jones."

Kat took her time studying the face that stared back at her from the other side of the dusty sitting room that she could never remember anyone actually sitting in. The man had white bushy eyebrows and dark brown eyes, and the smile that peeked out from behind the perfectly trimmed goatee was devious at best.

"I'm going to need to see some ID," she told him.

"Of course," he said with a laugh. He stepped forward and handed her a business card that read *Chamberlain & King Insurance and Underwriters, London, England*. When he added, "Here you go, my dear," and flashed a British passport, the picture was off, Kat thought. The accent, however, was spot on.

"So how do I look?" the man asked.

"Old," Gabrielle said, leaning closer as she applied theatrical make-up to the corners of his mouth. "But not old enough. And blotchy."

"But you sound good to me," Kat told him.

Only then did Hale smile. "I'm going to remember you said that."

"Sure thing, Ezra. Just tell me this: the real Mr Jones is..."

"Ecstatic." He looked again at the man's wallet. "It seems someone from Hale Industries met him at the airport this morning and offered him his dream job in the Cayman Islands. In fact, he called London from the Hale Industries jet and quit his old job just a half-hour ago."

"Shame his company's not gonna get the message," Gabrielle added.

"It is," Hale said with a solemn nod.

"And that he lost his wallet..." Kat went on.

Hale raised one false eyebrow. "A tragedy indeed." When he slid the small leather case into the inside pocket of his suit jacket, the two girls watched him. Kat had pulled aside the heavy drapes, and light streamed into the room, bouncing off faded dusty furniture, a cold fireplace and a perfectly forged Rembrandt that had hung above the mantelpiece for longer than Kat had been alive.

"Kat, what are we going to do about his shoulders?" Gabrielle tried to pull his arms down, but nothing about him seemed to move. "And that gut," she said, patting him on the stomach.

"Hey, I've never had any complaints in that area before," Hale said smugly.

"Exactly," Gabrielle cried. "Would it kill you to eat a muffin every now and then?"

Kat was biting her nails, walking around Hale, staring

him slowly up and down.

"His hands are off," Gabrielle pointed out.

"Posture's wrong," Kat said.

"He's still...hot," Gabrielle said, as if it were the greatest insult in the world.

"I feel so objectified. So...cheap," Hale told them, but the girls talked on.

"This would work from a distance, but in close quarters and under high scrutiny..." Kat let the thought trail off.

"Couldn't you have found someone younger?" Gabrielle said.

"It was a miracle I found *him*." Hale pointed to the documents on the table.

"We either need a young guy for you to impersonate or an old guy to do the impersonating!" Gabrielle threw her hands into the air. "We need—"

"No," Kat said before the words could even come out. "Uncle Eddie is not a part of this."

Gabrielle crossed her arms. "But he is the *ultimate* old guy."

"Maybe we should call him, Kat," Hale said. "I mean, where are we going to find a suitable old guy in twenty-four hours?"

"Excuse me, miss?"

Kat turned towards the soft voice and had to shake her head. For a second, she could have sworn she was seeing double. She looked between the photo of Ezra Jones that lay on the table and the way Marcus stood in the door. They had the same eyes, the same colouring, and the same look of people who have been orbiting around great wealth and power – always on the perimeter, always close enough to serve – for a lifetime.

Marcus drew a deep breath. "Your dinner is ready."

3 DAYS UNTIL
THE EMERALD ARRIVES

NEW YORK, NEW YORK
USA

SEVEN

The Cleopatra Emerald was not cursed – everyone at the Oliver Kelly Corporation for Auctions and Antiquities said so.

After all, an emerald – no matter how large – did not cause the ship carrying Oliver Kelly the First to sink in shallow waters off the coast of Nova Scotia. And once the stone was set in platinum and given to a railway heiress from Buenos Aires, there was no way any necklace – no matter how heavy – could force a woman to lose her head in a very tragic steam engine incident.

Of course, it was impossible to deny that the next owner went bankrupt. The small country that added the stone to its crown jewels was invaded. And the museum that displayed the Cleopatra for a short time was burned almost entirely to the ground.

But it wasn't cursed.

Everybody at the Kelly Corporation said so.

"It's not cursed, Mr Jones."

"Of course not." Hale gave a deep throaty laugh and slapped Marcus on the back. Marcus, as per their agreement, said nothing. "But, Mr Kelly, as the Cleopatra's insurer of record, Mr Jones is of the opinion that the stone would be best left exactly where it is."

"Excuse me." Kelly cut him off. "Who are *you*, exactly?"

"Well, as I said on the phone, Mr Kelly, I'm Colin Knightsbury. I'm Mr Jones's personal assistant."

Kelly seemed to consider this before turning and saying, "Fine."

Hale was not short, lazy or unathletic, and yet it felt somehow like a struggle to keep up, as they followed Oliver Kelly the Third down the polished halls and gleaming corridors. It didn't look like the sort of place that had its roots in shady places and black market deals, but if there was one thing every W. W. Hale learned early on, it's that you never *really* want to know where the money comes from.

"And as I said on the phone, we at Chamberlain and King believe that moving the Cleopatra on this schedule could be quite dangerous. If you could delay—"

Kelly came to an abrupt stop and wheeled on the pair. "I'm sure you *would* like me to delay, but seeing that it's my stone, I think I'll do with it as I please."

"Before his death," Hale started, "your father was adamant that the stone not be displayed in public, and—"

"My father inherited this company," Kelly snapped, gesturing to the people and things that filled the hall. "And do you know what he did with it?" he asked, but didn't wait for an answer. "Nothing, Mr Jones. He *maintained* what my grandfather had built – that's all. I don't expect you to understand what it's like to be in a family business, but the job of future generations is not to *maintain*. The one major decision my father made was to buy the Cleopatra back thirty years ago, and then he locked it up goodness knows where—"

"Switzerland," Hale said.

"What?"

"According to our records, the stone is in a high-security box in a Swiss bank."

"I know that," Kelly snapped, and pushed the elevator call button. "The point is that no one has seen it. I have never even seen it. It's the greatest asset this company has, and all it's done in thirty years is collect dust and wait for some mythical mate to turn up so that some ridiculous curse can be broken."

"Of course, of course," Hale said.

Kelly looked at him as if to say, *I was talking to your boss.*

That was when Hale slid closer. "You'll have to forgive Mr Jones, Mr Kelly," he confided softly as Marcus stood three steps behind them, stoic, silent as the grave. "He can see the smallest crack in a company's defences, the slightest fault. I'm here to make sure Mr Jones isn't distracted. The man's a genius, you see. And when Mr Jones says that it might be best to wait—"

There was a ding, and the elevator doors were sliding open.

"*My grandfather* was a genius," Kelly snapped. "A visionary."

Hale stepped inside the elevator, secretly wishing the man would have the nerve to add "*a thief*".

"That stone is the Kelly Corporation's signature piece," Kelly continued, "and it's not going to stay in a hole in the ground. Not on my watch."

The doors slid closed, and Hale couldn't help but study the reflection of Oliver Kelly the Third – the handmade suit and full-Windsor knot. Antique cuff links and Italian calfskin shoes, all of which had one purpose: to make sure no one ever mistook him for ordinary. All at the age of twenty-nine. Hale might not have hated him so much had it not been like looking in a fun-house mirror – at who he might have become if he hadn't been home two years before on the night when Kat came to steal his Monet.

"Yes, Mr Kelly," Hale said slowly, still taking the image in. "I understand completely."

"Good." When the elevator doors opened, Kelly turned and extended a hand towards Marcus. "Thank you for coming, Mr Jones. I appreciate your time. But as you can see, our paperwork is in order, and our security –" he gestured at the showroom on the main level of the building, its gleaming cases and cameras and guards – "is the best it can possibly be, so I'm afraid you've made the trip for nothing."

"Indeed." Hale reached to take the hand that was offered, held it a little longer than Kelly was perhaps expecting, squeezed it a little tighter. "What do you think, Mr Jones?"

Marcus let his gaze sweep around the room. His voice was stoic and cold when he said, "I think the last time I heard that was at the Henley."

Hale watched Oliver Kelly the Third shudder at the words. The colour faded from his cheeks, and his mouth drew into a thin hard line. "The Henley?"

"Oh yes," Hale said. "They assured us that no one could ever steal *Angel Returning to Heaven* from their walls, and we believed them. But we were all wrong on that account, weren't we, Mr Kelly?"

Honesty was a rare thing in Oliver Kelly's business. People negotiated. Dealers lied. He wasn't exactly sure what to do when faced with someone so willing to admit a mistake, so he didn't do anything – he just stood, waiting.

"And, of course, they thought their paperwork was in order too, and now..." Hale trailed off, then risked a glance at Oliver Kelly the Third. "Well, I'm afraid I'm not at liberty to comment, but let's just say they're still waiting for a cheque. And with a piece like the Cleopatra Emerald – with its cultural and monetary significance—"

"It's not cursed," Kelly said automatically.

"Of course not. But if you don't mind –" Hale placed his hands behind his back, smiled warmly – "Mr Jones would like to start with the basement."

"And the cameras on this level?" Hale asked twenty minutes later.

"The same as the level before," the director of security said from his place at Mr Kelly's right side.

Kelly watched as Hale took copious notes. He snapped hundreds of pictures.

"And these windows?" Hale asked. "They're monitored by...?"

"Glass break detectors at fifteen-yard intervals."

"Bulletproof?"

"Of course." The security director sounded almost offended.

"Excellent." Hale took yet another picture, then consulted his clipboard one more time. "Then I believe all that remains is the vault. The model number on that again is..."

"I'm sorry, Mr Jones," Kelly said, "but I distinctly remember providing that information in our quarterly report."

"Yes," Hale stepped in to answer. "And last quarter, the Cleopatra Emerald was scheduled to stay safely on the other side of the world, so forgive us if we visit the subject again." He turned to the security director. "The model on this door sensor..."

"Helix 857J," the man said with no emotion.

"I assure you, gentlemen," Mr Kelly interrupted again. "We at the Kelly Corporation know exactly how valuable our emerald is, and we have taken every precaution to protect—"

"*Your* emerald?" Hale tilted his head. "Does everyone agree about that?"

The man flushed. "Well, of course. Who else could..."

Hale turned to Kelly, stared straight into his eyes, and said, "Tell me about Constance Miller."

"The subject of Ms Miller is a matter for our legal department – not security. I can assure you that the Cleopatra's so-called history has no bearing on her safety."

"Yes." Hale smiled. "We heard *that* from the Henley too."

"Listen here, Mr..."

"Knightsbury," Hale provided, but Kelly talked on.

"Constance Miller is a recluse. She's old."

"Does she have friends?" Hale asked.

"Friends who could help her *steal* an *emerald?*" Kelly laughed as if it were the funniest thing he'd heard in ages. "I think not."

"Family?"

"Yes. A grandson, I think."

"Does she have a claim, sir?"

Kelly scoffed. "Not a legitimate one. The best courts in two countries have said so for a dozen years."

"Twelve years is a long time to want something, Mr Kelly."

"Yes, but—"

"A very long time to hear *no*."

But *no* was not a word that Oliver Kelly the Third had ever heard. To hear it for a dozen years seemed more than the young man could understand.

Kelly dropped his voice and finished, "Perhaps I should have my secretary put together a file."

"Yes." Hale smiled. "Perhaps you should."

"Excuse me, miss. May I help you?"

Kat didn't turn at the question. Two feet away, there was a case full of rubies and diamonds – a pendant rumoured to have belonged to Catherine the Great and a pair of earrings featured in a movie starring Audrey Hepburn. But those things didn't really matter to Kat. Kat was far more concerned about the one case that was empty.

"What goes in here?" she asked the salesman.

"Oh, I'm afraid that space is reserved for a very special— Don't do that," the man said when Kat propped one hand on the case (and fingered the hydraulic base and titanium stand with the other).

"But what *is* it?" Kat chomped her gum. "I might want to buy it, you know. I've got a birthday coming up, and my dad said I could pick out anything I want. Maybe I want what goes in here."

She tapped the glass (and surmised that it was drill-proof and at least an inch thick).

"I'm afraid it isn't for sale."

Kat rolled her eyes (and noted the positions of the surveillance cameras on the north wall). "Then what's it doing in a store if it's not for sale?"

"We are an auction house, young lady, and this is an exhibition piece that will be displayed until— Please don't do that," the man said, grabbing Kat's hand just as she reached beneath the case's edge, fingering the pressure-sensitive lip of the pedestal.

"Excuse me," Kat said when she bumped into a man who was browsing among the cases (and felt the telltale shoulder holster of a plainclothes guard).

"Miss," the salesman went on, "perhaps you would be more interested in our collection of—"

"So you're just going to show it off?" Kat scanned the

gleaming showroom floor (and noticed the state-of-the-art motion sensors at the pedestal's base).

"Yes, we are—"

"That doesn't seem very fair," Kat huffed. She took one last look around the room, at the guards and the cameras, the exits and the case, and then turned to leave.

"Miss," the salesman called, "I am sure there are many other things that will work with your price range." He swept his arm around the showroom floor.

"That's OK." In the corner of the room, an antique clock began to chime. "I think I've got everything I need."

"You're late."

Kat felt her cousin fall into step beside her, but didn't turn to look. She was probably the only person on the street that day not staring at the slender girl in the short trench coat and tall black boots, but that didn't really matter.

Gabrielle pointed to the Kelly catalogue in Kat's hands. "So can we do it?"

Kat took a deep breath and shoved the thin book into her pocket. "Right now, I'm more worried about whether or not we *should* do it." She eyed her cousin. "You got the key?"

Gabrielle rolled her eyes and flashed a small magnetic card from a hotel near Times Square. "Of course I got the key."

They could have picked the lock, rappelled down from the roof - maybe swiped a couple of maid uniforms and a housekeeping trolley for good measure - but Kat and Gabrielle were smart enough to know that the shortest distance between two points was always a straight line. Or a picked pocket, as the case may be.

So they made their way into the hotel lobby and lift without any fanfare or unnecessary risk. They were just two girls on their own in the big city – all the way to the small, modest room on the alley side of the seventh floor.

"So how was your day, Gabrielle?" Kat asked.

"Do you have any idea how hard it is to tail an eighty-year-old woman? It's hard. Really hard. Really...*slow*." Then Gabrielle raised a fist and knocked. "Housekeeping?" she called while Kat stood just out of view. "Housekeeping!" she tried again. After a long quiet beat, she used the key, and together the cousins stepped inside.

For all the hotel rooms that Kat had seen in her short life, she couldn't remember the last time she'd been in one like that. It consisted of nothing more than two full beds, a clean small bath, a desk, and one wardrobe with hangers permanently attached to the rod.

"Well, they travel like they're almost out of money," Gabrielle said, moving through the room so quickly and softly that Kat doubted her feet even made an impression in the carpet.

"How much time do we have?" Kat asked.

"They just went in with their lawyer, so let's call it forty minutes."

"Let's call it thirty," Kat countered, and Gabrielle shrugged – the universal signal for *Have it your way*.

It didn't really matter. They could have done what they

needed to do in ten. There was only the bedroom and bathroom, after all. The wardrobe held two suitcases that had probably been quite expensive fifty years before but were now faded and beaten; three pairs of shoes and an assortment of clothes that were worn but neatly mended – all with London labels.

"Found the safe," Gabrielle called from the cabinet that held the minibar. Inside was a small box that was standard issue for hotel chains around the world, so it only took a minute for Kat to crack it. A moment later, she was pulling out two passports in the names of Marshall and Constance Miller. Two hundred dollars in traveller's cheques. A family locket. And a beaten, weathered file about a very famous emerald and an almost-as-notorious court case.

Kat watched her cousin flip through page after page – black-and-white images of a family in the desert; photocopies of ancient ledgers written in a woman's elegant hand. And countless letters from Oliver Kelly the Third, urging Constance Miller to "move on", "give up", and finally, "get a real hobby."

"Oh," Gabrielle said slowly, "I really don't like this guy."

But it was the last page that made them stop – because it was the last page where someone had taped a plain white business card with simple black letters that spelled the name *Visily Romani.*

EIGHT

An hour later, Kat was alone in the middle of Madison Square Park, watching the fat white flakes that floated between the grey sky and the Kelly building – a nagging voice in the back of her mind telling her that something was about to go terribly wrong.

Maybe it was the location: high-security buildings are hard. High-security high-rises are suicide. Perhaps it was because the Kelly Corporation's cameras were state-of-the-art, and their security consultants used to cash pay cheques from places like the CIA.

It was not because of curses. It was not because of Hale. It was certainly not because Visily Romani – no matter how noble his motives – was developing an annoying habit of pulling Kat into jobs that far older and experienced (and some might even say *sane*) thieves would never dare attempt.

No – Kat shook her head against the thought, blinked away the snow that landed on her dark lashes – that wasn't it.

"If I didn't know any better," a strong voice said from behind her, "I'd say you were casing that joint."

Hale was there. Kat turned to see Gabrielle punch his arm and say, "Told you we'd find her here."

But there was nothing playful in the way Hale was looking at her as he said, "I should probably warn you that Oliver Kelly isn't messing around."

And that was when Kat knew there was no single part of this job that worried her – it was everything together. From the building, to the target, to the way Hale crossed his arms and studied her through the falling snow. But most of all, there was...

"Romani." Kat looked up at the grey sky. "They had Romani's card." She stood waiting for an answer of some kind, but got nothing. "So it's legit. So I think I've got to do this." She studied Hale through the falling snow. "So...say something."

"That place is a fortress, Kat."

"Romani wouldn't have sent Constance Miller to me if he didn't think I could—"

"*We*," Hale snapped.

"Of course. If he didn't think *we* could do it."

"I don't like it, Kat," Hale said, and just that quickly, Kat knew he was right.

"I don't like it either, but I think...I think I've got to try. You don't have to come with me if you—"

"No." Hale shook his head. "No way. If you're in, I'm in."

Together, the two of them turned to Gabrielle, who plopped onto a park bench and crossed her legs. "So what do we know?" She stared at the building in the distance as if trying to move it through the sheer power of her mind. It might have worked, too, if Hale hadn't stepped in front of her.

"The stone arrives Thursday from Switzerland via private charter. It will go immediately to the tenth floor, where it will be polished, verified and appraised."

"How long?" Kat asked.

Hale shrugged. "If they're not distracted, I'd say three hours. Maybe less."

Gabrielle looked at Kat. "Didn't the Wobbley Brothers do Humpty Dumpty once in three hours?"

"*Maybe less*," Hale said again, even louder.

"And it's cursed," Gabrielle chimed in. "What?" she asked when Kat gave her a look. "I'm just saying we should never underestimate curses."

"What about transit?" Kat asked, ignoring her.

Hale shook his head. "They've got three different armoured-car companies with three different routes, and that morning they'll flip a coin to see which one gets the job. Plus, once it's in transit, there's...you know...an armoured truck. And guards. With guns."

"The Bagshaws blew up an armoured truck once," Gabrielle offered.

"*And guards.*" Hale's voice rose even more. "What's the first floor like?" he asked, but Kat was already shaking her head.

"It's as good as you'd think it would be – maybe better. Four guards. Two uniforms at the front door, one at the staff

62

entrance, and a plainclothes that probably rotates, depending on the day."

"Cameras?" Hale asked.

"Lots."

"Blind spots?" Gabrielle said.

"None." Across the street, the lights were fading to black, and Kat saw the employees slipping from the door on the side of the building, disappearing among the commuters and workers and shoppers of midtown Manhattan.

"Night's no good," Kat said to their unasked question. "Even if we could get past the guards and security, the emerald's case sinks into a reinforced titanium vault beneath the floor at closing time."

"Basement access?" Hale asked, perking up.

"No." Kat shook her head. "With that kind of case, there won't be any access of any kind."

"How do you know?"

"Tokyo," Kat and Gabrielle said at the same time.

Gabrielle shrugged when Hale looked at her. "If you don't believe us, Uncle Felix has got the blowtorch scars to prove it."

Kat's gaze was lost in the distance, her voice low, and when she spoke, it was almost to herself, saying, "The stone is small, and small means easy to hide." Hale and Gabrielle stayed quiet, letting her talk, mind working, gears turning. "But no one's seen it in years, and if no one's seen it, then everyone's going to be staring, and staring people tend to...see. But staring also means focused, and focused people get scared, and scared people get distracted..."

"So we're back to Humpty Dumpty," Gabrielle tried, but Hale was already shaking his head.

"No," he said. "I'm telling you, even if we can get the king's horses in there, there's no way we make it *out* before someone notices the emerald is gone. And trust me, we do not want to be caught on the inside." He cringed. "Ex-Navy SEALs. Big ones."

When Kat spoke, it was more a hypothetical question than a challenge: "What if they don't notice?"

"No, Kat. No." Despite the snow, sweat was beading at Hale's brow. "I'm telling you, if we had a month and a big crew...maybe. But Kelly is not messing around with this thing. We don't have the time or the resources to—"

"What are you thinking?" Gabrielle asked, cutting him off.

"Kat!" Hale snapped, probably louder than he'd intended, because when he spoke again, the words were softer. Sadder. "Kat, Uncle Eddie couldn't steal it."

There it was – the single fact that was scarier than the guards, more worrisome than the cameras. It was the one thing that, no matter what, Kat knew she could never plan a way around. What they were talking about doing was forbidden; it went against her family and its rules, and so Kat didn't dare look at that job through Uncle Eddie's eyes. Instead, she looked at it like Visily Romani.

"The authentication room," Kat said, almost to herself. "We can do an Alice in Wonderland in the authentication room."

They stayed perfectly still in the wet air, the plan taking shape around them like puzzle pieces formed out of the falling snow. The three of them stood shaking from the cold and with the knowledge that maybe – just maybe – it might work. And maybe, Kat knew, it wouldn't.

Gabrielle stared into her cousin's eyes. "Whatever you do, Kat, just *do not* say we're gonna need a forger."

"No, Gabrielle. We're going to need someone who can fake the Cleopatra Emerald in seventy-two hours." Kat started walking. Her short hair blew across her face as she turned her head and called against the wind, "We're going to need *the* forger."

2 DAYS BEFORE
THE EMERALD ARRIVES

SOMEWHERE IN
AUSTRIA

NINE

"Do I know him?" Hale asked.

Together, the cousins said, "No."

Kat and Gabrielle sat together in the backseat of the huge SUV that Hale had paid for and Marcus drove. They swayed as the big tyres lunged in and out of the deep gouges in the rough road. No, Kat realised. On second thought, *road* was far from the appropriate word.

Path.

Trail.

Death trap?

The dense canopy of trees parted, and for a brief second, nothing but snow and sky stood between them and the sheer cliff with its steep drop. Gabrielle – one of the best high-wire workers to ever grace the family business – leaned close to the glass and peered into the white abyss.

Hale, on the other hand, looked as if he might be sick all over the SUV's soft leather interior. "So are we sure this guy will be there?"

Kat looked at the pristine snow that lay before them,

eighteen inches deep and completely untouched by man. "He's home," she said, certain that no one had been up – or down – that mountain in a very long time.

Marcus drove steadily faster. The tyres spun, and the SUV skidded; but still they kept their forward progress, climbing.

"And how do we know he'll be able to help us?" Hale asked, his voice an octave higher than Kat had ever heard it.

"Oh, he *can* help us." Maybe it was the change in Gabrielle's voice – the sudden inflection – or maybe Hale was just desperate to look anywhere but over the sharp cliff that Marcus was currently navigating, because he spun around and stared into the backseat.

"What does that mean?" Hale asked.

"It means...well..." Kat started, then stumbled, searching. "You see, by some standards he might be a little..."

"Weird." Gabrielle shrugged against her cousin's glare. "The man is ten pounds of kooky in a five-pound sack."

"He's *eccentric*," Kat tried.

"Bizarre."

"He's got something of an artist's temperament."

"I say a screw loose."

"He's a little...unpredictable."

But this time, there was no teasing as Gabrielle corrected, "No, Kat. The word is *banished*."

Kat felt the truth wash over them, silent and chilly as the snow. Then she shook her head. "So he and Uncle Eddie don't get along. That has nothing to do with his work. His work is good."

"I know, but if Uncle Eddie doesn't want anyone to use him—"

"Well, Uncle Eddie also says no one should steal the Cleopatra Emerald. Don't worry, Gabrielle. Not even Uncle Eddie can kill us twice," Kat said, turning back to the frosty glass.

"Oh, if anyone can..." Hale twisted and stared down the steep cliff again.

"Besides," Kat said as the SUV slowed, "we're here."

Marcus guided the car from the twisting road into a clearing, where the dense pines gave way to an even smaller lane, a low stone fence, and a tiny cabin with smoke spiralling into the sky. Icicles hung from the roof, and the whole thing might easily have been made out of gingerbread.

"Yeah," Hale said, staring out of the window. "He's got to be a criminal mastermind, all right."

Outside the SUV, the snow was up to Kat's knees, and she had to hold Hale's arm to steady herself as they waded their way through the deep drifts to the small shaded stoop.

"Hale," Kat said slowly, "one more thing you might want to know about Charlie..."

Gabrielle was ahead of them, her long legs skirting over the drifts like the wind.

"Yeah?" Hale said.

"He's Eddie's brother..."

"OK."

"And..."

71

Looking up at Hale, Kat had to think that the sky was so clear, so blue, so close. Hale was close. He felt *with her*, and she honestly didn't know whether or not that scared her – what she should or should not say. For a moment, there didn't seem to be anything to say at all.

But just as quickly, that moment was over, because the door was swinging open, a gruff voice was saying, "Who's there?" and the three of them were turning, staring at the familiar face of Uncle Eddie.

"Kat?" She heard the worry in Hale's voice and knew he was already formulating cover stories and concocting lies.

"It's OK, Hale. He's—"

"Hello, Uncle Charlie." Gabrielle pushed her sunglasses onto the top of her head, and the wind blew through her long hair. She was beautiful – Kat could see it. And yet one of the best artists in the world seemed to barely notice. He was too busy staring past her, squinting against the glare of the sun that bounced off the snow – a blinding white.

"Nadia." His voice cracked and his lips quivered, but his gaze stayed locked on Kat. The best hands in the business were shaking as they pointed towards her.

"No, Charlie. This is Nadia's daughter, Kat. Remember?" Gabrielle whispered. "Nadia's gone, Charlie."

"Of course she is," the man snapped, and straightened and pulled back from the door. "Come inside if you're coming."

Kat and Hale stood alone in the sun, watching the old man disappear into the shadow of the house, and that was when Hale mumbled, "Uncle Eddie's got a twin... There are *two* Uncle Eddies."

"No." Kat shook her head. "There aren't."

False walls and fake IDs, frames with forged paintings, necklaces with imitation gems. Kat was well aware that most things in her world were a little bit unreal, but it had never seemed so obvious until she stood on the threshold of the tiny cottage at the top of the world. She thought of Mr Stein's house in Warsaw, entire rooms dedicated to the search for treasures that were gone, hidden, lost - perhaps never to be seen again. But Uncle Charlie's house...Charlie's house was the opposite in almost every way.

Three Mona Lisas hung beside the doorway. The mantel over the fireplace held at least a dozen Fabergé eggs. There was a basket of bearer bonds by the fire with the rest of the kindling, a set of hand towels in the bathroom that, had they not been made from terry cloth, would have been, collectively, an exact replica of Leonardo's *Last Supper*.

It was the oddest sort of museum that any of them had ever seen, so they turned slowly, taking the whole sight in.

"Forgive the mess," Charlie said, pushing aside a pile of canvases to clear a place on a faded wingback chair. "Haven't had company in a few days."

Or years, Kat thought, remembering the long snowy drive. She stood quietly, watching Hale's gaze sweep over the room, waiting for his eventual, "Um...Charlie?"

The old man jumped a little at the sound of his own name,

but still managed to mutter, "What?"

"Is that a real Michelangelo?" Hale pointed to a sculpture that sat in the corner, covered with hats and scarves and dust.

"Of course it is." Charlie patted the sculpture on the back. "Nadia helped me steal it."

Gabrielle and Hale seemed almost afraid to look at Kat then, as if the mention of her mother's name might be too much for her. Only Charlie seemed immune to the silence.

"Now *that's* one of mine." He pointed to the Rembrandt on the wall, dusty and old and perfectly identical to the one that had hung above Uncle Eddie's fireplace all of Kat's life. The original didn't matter. Not to Kat. Not when there were two perfect forgeries hanging a few thousand miles apart, like a portal linking two totally different worlds. When Kat looked at Charlie's painting, she tried to see how it might differ from its twin, but the differences were not a matter of canvas or paint. The differences, Kat knew, were in the paintings' lives.

"You look just like your mother."

Kat jerked, her uncle's voice pulling her back into the room and the moment. She felt her eyes begin to water and knew she wasn't the only one seeing double.

"Yeah." Kat wiped her eyes and hoped no one noticed. "I guess I do."

When Kat moved towards him, she thought that he might bolt and run, but instead he caught her arm and held her there. His hands were covered with varnish and stain – an artist's hands. Unburned and unscarred. And yet he just squeezed harder, tighter than a vice. There was something real about the master forger when he stared into her eyes and said, "Does he know you're here?"

Kat shook her head. "*No.*"

When he released Kat's arm and dropped into a chair, Gabrielle grabbed a footstool and pulled it closer. "Uncle Charlie," she started, "we have a job – a big one."

"*You* have a job?" he asked, then laughed, quick and hard. "Where's your mother?" he chided.

"She's busy," Gabrielle told him. "And we've pulled plenty of jobs on our own."

"I don't suppose you heard about the Henley?" Hale said, but his smooth smile broke when faced with Charlie's glare.

"Beginner's luck," the old man countered.

"We can do this, Uncle Charlie." For the first time in her life, Gabrielle sounded like someone who genuinely needed someone else's approval. "We've got a plan."

"You're children," the old man hissed.

"Like Nadia was a child?" Gabrielle said. "And my mother. And—"

"Don't touch that," Charlie snapped, and Hale inched away from the Ming vase that held an assortment of ratty old umbrellas.

"We came a long way to see you, Charlie," Gabrielle said.

The old man cut his eyes at her. "The ride is always easier on the way down."

"We wouldn't have come if there was anything in this world you couldn't make," Gabrielle said, not flirting; not lying. It was in no way a con when she told him, "We wouldn't be here if we didn't need the best."

"I am the best." It was the sure and steady voice of someone who knows that it's true. And yet, Kat couldn't help but notice that he rocked slightly at the waist. The artist's hands trembled. "I'm retired," he said, looking away. "And your uncle doesn't want you here."

"*You're* our uncle too," Gabrielle protested just as Kat eased onto the stool and caught her uncle's eyes.

"Someone is using one of the Pseudonimas, Uncle Charlie," she said, and watched him turn as pale as the snow. "Have you heard that?"

"It's not me," he snapped.

"I know." Kat reached for his hand, but he flinched and pulled away. "I know," she said again, softer this time. "But I need your help, you see."

"*We*," Hale inserted.

"*We* need to do a job for Visily Romani." Kat took a deep breath. "We need the Cleopatra Emerald."

And in a flash they were there – the steely resolve and power of will that Kat had seen so often on the face of Uncle Eddie. "No!" the man snapped, rising from the chair and pushing across the room with so much force Kat almost lost her balance.

She struggled to her feet, but the man didn't stop, didn't turn as Kat went on.

"The Kelly Corporation is moving the emerald to its corporate headquarters in New York two days from now, and we have to steal it, Uncle Charlie. Visily Romani needs *us* to steal it."

"No one *has* to steal the Cleopatra Emerald. Eddie knows that. We know that. We know... We learned that lesson the hard way." He turned to Gabrielle. "You should go."

"Charlie, please." Despite her smaller than average size, Kat crossed the room in three long strides.

"I can't make that in... It can't be... I'd need..."

"I'll get you whatever you need," Hale said.

"It cannot be done!" The old man yelled so loudly that Kat half feared an avalanche. "I can't make that. I can't make it. I can't..."

"We don't need you to make us a fake Cleopatra Emerald, Uncle Charlie." Kat's voice was low and kind and even. When she touched his arm, he didn't pull away. "We just need you to give us the one you've already got."

1 DAY BEFORE
THE EMERALD ARRIVES

BROOKLYN, NEW YORK
USA

TEN

Somewhere between the airport and the brownstone, the others must have fallen asleep. Kat watched Gabrielle curl into a tiny ball like a kitten while Hale splayed across the limo's backseat, long legs and arms, and a head that, on occasion, would drift onto Kat's shoulder in a way she couldn't bring herself to mind.

Kat knew that she should be resting, but her eyes stayed open, watching the darkness fade. Thinking. Planning. Worrying about all the ways it could end badly. The switch could get blown or the gear could jam. The roof access might be compromised and the blueprints could be out of date. There were always a million ways a job could go wrong, but only one way for it to go right.

There were always too many chances.

When the car stopped, the street was quiet in that space that wasn't quite night and wasn't quite morning, and the girl who wasn't quite a thief thought for a minute about staying there, telling Marcus to cut the engine and let everyone just sleep. But then Hale shifted beside her.

"We home?" Kat felt his breath against her neck, warm and soft. It was as if, half awake, he'd forgotten to be angry about Moscow and Rio and all the others. She missed the boy who was curled against her. "Did you sleep?"

"Sure."

"Liar," Gabrielle said, straightening and stretching. "You're thinking about the roof, aren't you?"

"Among other things," Kat had to admit.

"The switch?" Hale asked.

"The cameras?" Gabrielle guessed, but Kat sat perfectly still, unsure whether she was hearing the spinning of the wheels in her head or the idling car. It seemed to take all the strength she could summon to reach for the door and step out into the dusky light.

"The timing." She felt the green stone in her pocket, smooth and fragile. "The timing...is everything."

Turning from the car, Kat expected to see the empty street and the vacant brownstone, to find peace and quiet and anything but the sound of a gruff voice saying, "I couldn't have said it better myself."

Kat would never know how many faces and names her uncle had worn in his long life. Eddie himself probably had no idea. There was only one Eddie that mattered, though, and that was the man who turned and left the porch, walking through the dim house. That was the man the three teens followed into the heat of the kitchen.

"You'll sit," he told Kat. "You'll eat."

It was the first time in a long time that Kat could remember a decision being made for her, and she couldn't help herself – she did exactly as she was told. And she liked it.

He struck a match and lit the flame on the old stove, then pulled a dozen eggs from the refrigerator. It was part habit, part ritual, and the hands that had run a thousand cons moved with steady, even purpose.

"You have been to Europe."

It wasn't a question, and Kat knew better than to deny it. Hale and Gabrielle shared a worried glance behind her uncle's back, but Kat just sat, feeling the weight of Charlie's stone in her pocket, pressing against her hip.

"And how is your Mr Stein?"

The first thought that came to Kat's mind was relief: *He doesn't know.* The second, she had to admit, was irritation. "He's not *my* Mr Stein."

"I see headlines about statues in Brazil..." Uncle Eddie talked on as if she hadn't spoken at all. "I hear whispers that a Cézanne has gone missing in Moscow..."

Hale held up two fingers. "Just a little one."

"And I think maybe the South American operation can survive a few days without me. I think maybe I am needed at home."

Eddie found his cast-iron frying pan but didn't turn, didn't speak, until the silence was too much for Kat, and she blurted, "They were easy jobs."

Uncle Eddie looked at Hale, who shrugged and said, "I wouldn't know." He leaned against the wall and crossed his arms. "Wasn't invited."

Kat felt an odd thing in the air then, with Uncle Eddie looking at Hale. "She goes alone?" her uncle asked.

"She's slippery that way," Hale said, and suddenly Kat hated them for whatever alliance they had formed in her absence.

"*She* is standing right here!" Kat snapped. "The last I checked, *she* has managed everything she's tried so far."

"Talent, Katarina, is a dangerous thing." Uncle Eddie turned back to his stove, placed bacon onto cast iron, and when he spoke again, it was in Russian, low and under his breath.

"What was that?" Hale asked.

"'The man who loves the wire needs the net,'" Gabrielle translated, then read Hale's blank expression. "It means—"

"Leave us," Eddie told Hale and Gabrielle.

"But..." Gabrielle pointed to the frying pan and the bacon and the eggs.

"Now," Eddie snapped, and a second later Kat was alone at the kitchen table.

There was no doubt the room was different. Uncle Eddie might have been back at his stove, but his absence was everywhere – from the calendar that hadn't been changed, to the suitcase by the door. But the only thing that really mattered to Kat was the newspaper that lay on top of all the others, the same headline still screaming in the room, calling out for all to see that the Cleopatra was on the move.

"We are very much alike, Katarina."

It should have been a compliment, the highest praise. Kat could think of at least a dozen people who had been working for those very words their whole lives, but not Kat. Kat knew there was far more to the story.

"I was once a brilliant young thief...who wasn't nearly as brilliant as I thought." He took a deep breath. "It is a shame to see history repeat itself."

"Excuse me?" Kat rose to her full height and then regretted it. It felt like far too little, far too late.

"It seems as if you don't approve of the family business, Katarina." He shrugged. "Or of me. But these chances you take...these things you do...this is a dangerous life to live...alone."

Kat couldn't help herself; she thought about Rio and Moscow and the look in Gabrielle's eyes when she'd warned that a person can get drunk on this life – on these highs – and when that happens, Kat knew, there was bound to be a long, long way to fall.

But Kat was smart and careful, and there was not a doubt in her mind when she stepped towards him, threw her arms out wide, and said, "Look at where I am, Uncle Eddie. I'm back. I'm here. And I'm not alone."

"Yes." There was something sad in the word. "You're here. When it suits you."

"Do you not like *how* I'm stealing? Or do you not like *why*?"

"Listen to me, Katarina—"

"What kind of thief do you want me to be, Uncle Eddie? What *should* I steal – whatever it is in Uruguay?"

"Paraguay," her uncle corrected.

The newspaper lay on the table, staring at Kat - calling to her like a dare. "Oh, hey." She reached for it. "I see the Cleopatra Emerald is coming to town. Maybe I'll make a play for that."

Kat had no idea why she'd said it, but the words were already out there - too late to take them back. Maybe she wanted her uncle to forbid it. Maybe she expected him to laugh - as if the idea were far too absurd. But instead he reached for the paper and tossed it among the eggshells and coffee grounds with the rest of the rubbish.

"We do not joke of such a thing."

"I know," Kat said, but Uncle Eddie was already turning.

"The Cleopatra Emerald is no plaything!"

"I know," she said, trying to make him understand, but it was too late.

"You're a smart girl, Katarina - too smart to take stupid chances. Better thieves than you have gone after that blasted stone, and they have paid." He stopped, and Kat could have sworn she saw his hand shake. His lips were a thin hard line when he whispered, "Great thieves have paid dearly."

Kat's voice was different when she said, "I know."

"We do not steal the Cleopatra, Katarina. It is..." Eddie trailed off, struggling for words.

"Cursed," Kat offered.

Eddie turned to her. He shook his head. "*Forbidden.*"

On the stove, grease was popping, and smoke was rising from the frying pan, filling the room. It was the first time in

Kat's life that she had ever seen her uncle burn the bacon, so she stayed quiet, thinking of all the things she could not say.

"If you don't want to be like the rest of us, Katarina, then you should go back to school. You should leave this world – really leave us all behind. Don't let this old man stand in your way."

Kat wasn't going to cry. Her voice wasn't going to crack. "I came back, Uncle Eddie. Last year, after the Henley, I could have gone to any school in the world – I could have done anything, but I came back."

"You ran away, Katarina."

"And now I'm back."

It should have been an easy thing to prove, a fact to verify. She wanted him to say, *Good work, nice job* – to tell her that he was proud to have her at his kitchen table – but instead he turned back to the bacon and the stove.

"You're still running."

The kitchen was too hot – the big house suddenly too small. Her uncle's words were too loud, ringing in her ears, and Kat knew she couldn't stay there. Outside, the early morning air would be cool and fresh, so she didn't even stop for her jacket; she didn't look for her purse. She just moved down the long hall to the door without another thought or worry or fear. Outside. She'd be able to think outside.

"He's right, you know."

Kat stopped at the sound of the voice. Her hand was on the doorknob, freedom just inches away, but it was like she'd forgotten how to unlock a door when she turned and saw Hale sitting alone at the top of the stairs.

"I thought – after the Henley – you were back with us." He looked down at his hands. "With me. But now—"

"I don't need another lecture, Hale." Kat's hands were shaking. Her lips were trembling. It was as if her own body were against her. "I don't need someone else telling me what to do."

"Oh, no one tells you what to do, Kat. *You're* the girl who robbed the Henley."

"Yeah," Kat told him. "And I—"

"But you didn't do it alone." He stood and started slowly down the stairs.

"I know that."

"Do you?" Hale laughed. "Do you really? Because it seems to me like you've forgotten a lot of things."

It was the eve of the biggest job of her life, and Kat didn't have time to doubt or room to think. Gabrielle was right, Kat realised: boys are a lot less trouble when they're on the other side of the world.

"I'm sorry, Hale. I'm sorry I didn't take you to Moscow. Or Rio. I'm sorry I don't have time to hold your hand and stroke your ego. But I don't. And if you don't like it, here's the door."

"You're right. Maybe I should leave." He stepped towards her, backing her slowly into the shadows of the corner. "But maybe you should leave too – just walk away. Forget the Cleopatra and disappear."

It felt to Kat as if, all at once, the world was moving way too fast. Her mind raced, and Hale eased closer.

"We don't have to do this," he told her. "Just say the word and I can have a jet here in an hour. We can go anywhere." His warm hands wrapped around her fingers, so that they melted like ice. "We can do anything. We don't have to do *this*."

Charlie's stone felt heavy in Kat's pocket, pressing into her skin. She thought of Romani and Mr Stein, of sand and sun and the thieves like Oliver Kelly the First – the worst kinds of criminals, the ones who steal fortunes and respectability, both, somewhere along the way.

"Just say the word, Kat. Say any word."

Kat took a deep breath and pushed away. She didn't let herself look back as she opened the door and said the word "Romani".

THE DAY THE EMERALD ARRIVES

NEW YORK, NEW YORK
USA

ELEVEN

It stands to reason that, through the years, the people in the New York office of the Oliver Kelly Corporation for Auctions and Antiquities had become more or less immune to pretty things.

The back room held a sceptre that had been part of the crown jewels of Austria. Every day at four p.m., the director of antiquities sipped tea from a service that had once belonged to Queen Victoria herself. So to presume that incredible beauty was incredibly rare would be incorrect indeed. But on that Friday morning, no one would have known it.

The women wore their highest heels, the men their most expensive ties. As Oliver Kelly the Third walked down the gleaming, polished halls, the entire building pulsed as if Cleopatra herself were about to pay a visit.

"Well, there's the man of the hour."

Kelly turned at the voice. "Oh. Hello, Mr..."

"Knightsbury," Hale said, gripping Kelly's hand. "It's nice to see you again. Big day. Big day."

"Indeed," Kelly said with an impatient look at his watch.

"I presume Mr Jones is here to...oversee the transfer?"

"Oh, no, sir," Hale said. "Mr Jones was so impressed with your security that he sent me along with one of our junior associates. This is Ms Melanie McDonald. Ms McDonald has just joined the team. Since company policy dictates that two employees must witness—"

"Hello." That's when it became utterly obvious that even though Oliver Kelly the Third was accustomed to great beauty, tea sets and sceptres were no match for Gabrielle. "It's so nice to meet you, Ms McDonald," he said.

"Call me Melanie." Gabrielle extended one delicate hand. "It's so very nice to meet you, too."

There were at least a dozen people crowded in the halls. Gemologists and Egyptologists in white coats and tweed jackets; lawyers and very large men with very large guns strapped into shoulder holsters beneath the blazers of subpar suits.

Hale looked at the crowd, but not Kelly. Kelly simply looked at Gabrielle.

"Well, shall we go?"

Of all the pristine places inside the Kelly Corporation that day, Hale couldn't help but think that the room they saw next would make most hospitals jealous.

A stainless-steel table sat beneath bright lights. Assorted tools lay across cotton towels. There were microscopes and lasers, goggles and gloves. Every single person in the very crowded room stood in total silence as the doors opened and four uniformed guards entered, surrounding a man with a red bow tie and the thickest glasses Hale had ever seen. The wooden box he carried was small, and yet when he placed it in the centre of the steel table, he sighed as if it held the weight of the world itself.

"Have you met my cousin Pandora?" Gabrielle whispered to Hale. She gestured to the centre of the room. "*That* is her box."

People should have noticed, but no one heard anything beyond the squeak of the rusty hinges. And not a soul – not the appraisers or the guards – not even Oliver Kelly the Third himself could do anything but watch as the director of antiquities, in his crisp bow tie and white cotton gloves, reached into the box...

And retrieved the most valuable green stone that the world had ever known.

Hale had seen pictures, of course. He was a well-travelled young man, an educated child of means. A thief. Everyone who was at least one of those three things had seen pictures. But pictures did not capture the essence that comes with ninety-seven carats of pure, flawless green the colour of Ireland in springtime.

Curse or no curse, the man was right to hold the stone gently as he moved it to the table. The experts rotated around the emerald like planets circling the sun, scanning, measuring, and weighing – working wordlessly. It was almost like a dance, Hale thought. Like a con.

Beyond the hushed questions and answers of the experts, no one spoke until ninety minutes later, when a short woman

– the leading gemologist in the world, flown in from India for the occasion – stepped away from the stone and wiped her brow, and Oliver Kelly said, "Well?"

The whole room waited, watched as the woman cleaned her glasses and said, "Congratulations, Mr Kelly, this is the new home of the Cleopatra Emerald."

She held the stone towards its owner and motioned to the velvet-covered pillow on which it was supposed to sit. "Would you like to do the honours?"

If anyone expected Kelly to rush to take it, they were disappointed. Instead, he stood staring at the massive piece of green as if he had been secretly hoping it was a forgery.

A fake Cleopatra Emerald, after all, had never hurt anyone.

"Mr Kelly?" the woman asked again.

"Oh, it's beautiful," Gabrielle spoke at Kelly's side. "I can't imagine holding such a thing."

Kelly laughed. "Well, now's your chance..." He motioned for her to go ahead and take the emerald – to take history, quite literally, in the palm of her hand.

It wasn't an act, Hale knew, when Gabrielle reached carefully for the stone and looked as if she'd been waiting for that moment her entire life.

It almost broke his heart to have to say, "Again, Mr Kelly, I must remind you that the Cleopatra Emerald is a high-profile target."

"I know that," Kelly snapped.

"And we at Chamberlain and King would hate to see you take unnecessary chances with a stone of such...unique...

cultural significance. Its propensity for...shall we say... coinciding with unfortunate events and—"

"It's not cursed!" the man insisted one final time with entirely too much force. He swung his right arm, gesturing wildly, completely unaware of Gabrielle, who was walking past, hands outstretched, with the Cleopatra Emerald resting gently on her palms.

When Kelly's arm crashed into her, she stumbled onto the polished floor and watched the emerald tumble out of her hands. Shame and terror filled her face as she lunged after the stone, sliding, calling, "I'll get it! I'll—"

But her hand struck the stone again, sending it skidding towards a small vent that no one in the history of the Kelly Corporation had probably ever seen. But by then it was too late, and Oliver Kelly the Third, the director of antiquities, and the authentication department – not to mention the greatest experts in the world – had no choice but to watch as the most precious emerald in history disappeared.

Only Hale and Gabrielle seemed to be capable of moving. Together they rushed to the small vent that opened into a larger shaft that ran to the roof.

Hale leaned down. "I think I can reach it," he said, rolling up his sleeve, but Gabrielle was already on the floor beside him, her long thin arm reaching easily into the tiny space and grappling in the darkness for what felt like an eternity.

The lights still shone brightly in the pristine room, but it was as if a shadow covered them all as they thought about how emeralds can be easily scratched or chipped.

As they thought about curses.

But then the girl moved, and smiled, and pulled her hand from the grate – a gorgeous green stone clutched tightly in her grasp. It was covered with dust and cobwebs, but it was uncracked and unharmed.

And, of course, completely fake.

There was a lot that the people of the Kelly Corporation would never know about the Cleopatra Emerald. Like how it had truly come to Oliver Kelly so many years ago. Most likely, very few could comprehend the humiliation and pain that it had brought to the thieves of the world ever since.

And on the day of the Cleopatra's grand public return, no one would ever know about its very private exit through a dirty air vent, via a very thin cable and a dark-haired girl who kept the stone clutched tightly in her small hand, as she rose steadily towards the roof and the light.

TWELVE

There are several lessons every thief learns early on. Or dies.

Never turn your back on an angry guard dog (no matter how nice he seemed on your scouting trip). Don't leave home without a spare set of batteries (regardless of the guarantee you got from the guy at the store). And never, ever get attached to anything more valuable than you are.

Katarina Bishop was an excellent thief, and she had learned these lessons well, but riding through Midtown Manhattan in the back of a long black limousine, she couldn't stop thinking that the people who had made that last rule had never touched the Cleopatra Emerald.

"Do you want to hold it?" she asked, dangling the padded envelope in front of Hale with two fingers.

"No."

"Do you want to touch it and kiss it and wear it around your neck?"

"Don't be silly," he told her. "Everyone knows green isn't my colour."

Gabrielle had been right, Kat realised. There is a rush – a

thrill - that comes after a hard job, and Kat couldn't help herself. She'd held that green stone with her bare hands, and now she was drunk on adrenaline, high on life.

"You -" she scooted close - "were fabulous." She placed her head on Hale's chest and stared into the distance. "I see great potential in you...Wyatt?" He should have laughed; he should have teased, and when he didn't, she bolted upright. "Is that it? Is your name Wyatt?"

He gripped her arms and held her there, staring into her eyes as he said, "No."

Then Kat laughed and tossed back her head. "We did it, Hale."

Suddenly, she couldn't stay still. She wanted to stick her head out of the sunroof and scream, roll down the centre divider and tell Marcus to drive and drive and drive - she didn't care where. They could go anywhere - do anything - and for the first time in a long time, Katarina Bishop stopped thinking. And maybe that was why she found herself climbing onto her knees.

"We. Did. It!" she screamed, and when the car jolted to a stop, Kat didn't care that she was falling, landing across Hale's lap. She didn't think twice about the way her arms fell around his neck. When her lips found his, she didn't pull back, she just pressed against him, sinking into the kiss and the moment until...

The high was over. Kat jerked back, two thoughts pounding in her mind, screaming, *I kissed Hale.*

But it was the second thought that made her panic:

Hale didn't kiss me back.

"Sorry. I..." She sat up straight, and when she moved, she kicked something on the floorboard, looked down, and saw the bag that sat at his feet.

"What's that?"

"Paraguay."

She felt her heart sink. It was harder than it should have been to say, "It's smaller than I thought it would be."

She waited for Hale to laugh and tell her that it wasn't a very good joke. She wanted him to do anything but reach for the bag and pull it easily onto the seat beside him.

"Eddie says they need all the help they can get. I'm gonna head down there now that we're finished." He stopped. He didn't look at her when he asked, "*Are we finished?*"

Kat knew there was more to the question – that there was something else she was supposed to say. But Kat had always been good at telling lies. The truth, she realised, was a much harder thing to part with.

"You were right, Kat." There was a weight to Hale's voice. A gravity. "I should go."

Don't go.

"I know you still have to deliver the package, but...it's not like you need me."

But maybe I want you.

His hand was resting on the door handle. He took a deep breath and moved.

"Hale—"

"You could come," he said, spinning towards her.

The rush she'd felt before turned to panic, and Kat was frozen, no clue what to do or say.

"Your dad's already there. Gabrielle says Irina is coming. I mean, I know it's no Cleopatra job, but you could come. You could come if you wanted to."

"I want to, but I don't...steal...any more, Hale."

His voice was part whisper, part sigh, as he turned to the window and said, "You could have fooled me."

Before Kat could protest, Hale was reaching for a button on the limo door and saying, "Marcus." The car slowed and the centre partition slid down. "Take her wherever she wants to go."

"Hale, wait!" She reached for him, but the car stopped, and he was already opening the door, stepping out onto the busy pavement.

"You be careful out there." He pulled the large duffel bag onto his shoulder as if it weighed nothing at all. "I mean it, Kat. Take care."

Her hand was in his, resting gently. "Hale..."

"Goodbye, Kat." His voice was almost lost against the sound of honking cars and distant sirens. And just that quickly, he was gone. Out onto the street, coat collar turned up, disappearing into the traffic and the crowds.

It did not look like a clandestine rendezvous, not with the old woman and young man on the park bench and the teenage girl walking towards them, looking as if she'd just lost her very best friend.

"Is it true?" the woman asked.

The first time Kat had seen her, she'd guessed her age at somewhere over eighty, but that day Constance Miller looked younger by at least ten years. Maybe twenty. Her face was full of something. Kat breathed out, watched her breath fog in the chilly air, and knew that something was hope.

"Do you have it?" Constance Miller asked. "Is that why you called?"

"No, Grandmother. A theft like that would have been on the television." The man reached awkwardly for the old woman's hand.

"TV is overrated," Kat said, pulling the envelope from her pocket and tossing it onto the man's lap.

He stared down as if it were a tiny bomb and might explode. Only the woman dared to reach for it – carefully, tentatively.

"Is it really..."

"You can look," Kat said, glancing at the two uniformed police officers who stood twenty feet away, sipping coffee. "But I wouldn't touch."

"Oh, I believe you," the woman said, grabbing up the package and holding it tightly against her chest. "It's in here. I know it. I can feel it," she said, and Kat knew she wasn't talking about the weight or shape of the heavy stone in the padded envelope. She hadn't felt it with her fingers – she could feel it in her soul. Kat knew that sensation. She'd found it once on a school bus in London with four priceless paintings. She had seen it in Mr Stein's eyes every time she returned one of the missing Holocaust pieces to him so he could take it on the final leg of its journey home.

"Oh, thank you, Katarina. Thank you. If it hadn't been for you and Mr Hale—" The woman stopped and looked around. "Where's your friend?"

Kat couldn't help herself; she looked too.

"I'm afraid he had another obligation."

"Oh," Constance Miller said. "Do thank him for me, please. I just can't tell you how much..." But the words got caught.

"Grandmother, are you all right?" The young man's hand was on the woman's shoulder as it shook and she cried, clutching the precious package to her heart.

"I'm fine," the woman choked out. "I'm perfect."

The job was over. Her work was done. So Kat turned and started through the park.

"Katarina," the woman called one last time, and Kat stopped and turned back to the priceless gem she'd just stolen and given away without a second thought. "Thank you, Katarina. Thank you," the woman said, and Kat couldn't help but notice that the tears were gone. It was a different sort of smile. "We never could have done this without you."

Kat had often heard it said that asking a good thief to stop thinking would be like asking a shark to stop swimming, so she couldn't help herself as she walked away from the park that day, through the coming dusk of the city streets.

But that didn't mean she didn't try.

She didn't want to remember the feeling of the stone in her hand or the air rushing past her, zooming towards the light at the end of the shaft. She had absolutely no desire to think about Hale and her father and Paraguay. Or Uruguay. But more than anything, Kat, a girl who had been good at most things she'd ever tried, did not wish to entertain the notion that she might simply be a truly heinous kisser.

No. Kat shook her head. She wasn't going to think about that.

Not when there was a Klimt in Cairo and a Manet somewhere in Spain. Not when Mr Stein had left her a message regarding a long-lost Matisse that might be surfacing any day somewhere on the Mexican Riviera.

She wasn't going to think about how much colder it was when Hale's arm didn't periodically drape across her shoulder, when his broad shoulders weren't there to block the wind. She was the last person to care about Paraguay – or Uruguay – and whatever it was her family had decided to steal.

No, Kat had more than enough work to do on her own, she told herself, walking a little faster, feeling a little surer. She was starting to consider calling Mr Stein and making her next plan when she passed by a bar and heard the clink of glasses and the blaring television inside.

"The Cleopatra Emerald is one of the most famous gems in the world," the anchorwoman was saying. "Famous for its size, its tragic legend, and – more recently – the drama that has followed it into the courts of the world. The private woman behind one of the most public court battles of recent years joins us tonight for her very first interview. Constance Miller, thank you for being here."

And that was when Kat stopped. The world around her seemed to freeze as she stood, listening to the story of how Constance Miller's father and mother and *not* Oliver Kelly the First had found that stone among the sands of Egypt. She'd heard the story before, of course. Once in legend, and once from a woman in the back of a diner in the rain. And now she heard it again, from a woman with a tweed jacket and a British accent.

From a woman whom Kat had *never* seen before.

It wasn't really an earthquake, Kat was certain. And yet it felt as if the buildings were shaking. She stood stock-still in the flow of the pavement. People washed over her like the tide, and yet she didn't move.

"Excuse me," someone said, brushing against her, but Kat didn't register the words. She didn't feel a thing. Her mind was still hearing the same story from two faces, knowing at least one of them was a lie. A con.

Her phone rang, but the sound was coming from the other side of the world. Kat felt like she was moving in slow motion when she put her hand into her pocket and found the simple white card with the plain black letters that spelled the name *Visily Romani*.

With one touch, Kat knew it was different from the card she and Gabrielle had seen in the Millers' hotel room. The paper was softer, the lettering thicker. And there was no doubt in Kat's mind that *this* card was real. Despite her training – her blood – Katarina Bishop couldn't help but shiver as she turned the card over to read the handwritten words: *Get it back.*

THIRTEEN

Standing at the threshold of the Brooklyn brownstone, Kat watched the light from the street drifting down the long narrow hall that led from the front stoop to the ancient kitchen. She knew what she'd find inside: the old staircase and office, the sitting room and a powder bath. Kat saw it all with her thief's eyes. She knew which floorboards moaned and which door hinges squeaked, and yet she stood for a long time, staring into her great-uncle's home as if it were the one place on earth she no longer had the right to tread. It felt as if a laser grid lay inside. A minefield. But also, answers.

And what Kat really needed was answers.

"Uncle Eddie!" she called into the dark house. The card was in her pocket and her heart was in her throat, pounding. She swallowed hard and tried again. "Uncle Eddie!"

She crept past the sitting room, where no one ever sat, and down the hall, but the kitchen was empty and the stove was off and Kat knew without looking any further that her uncle wasn't there. She felt alone in the big house, trying to decide what to do. If Uncle Eddie had been there, he could have told her to sit or run, to eat or to cry. She wanted someone to do her thinking for her because she didn't trust her own mind any more. So she stood in the hallway, her thoughts on a constant loop, thinking...

I got conned.

I got conned.

I got...

"Kat?"

Kat jumped. The lights flickered on, and Kat spun to take in the boy behind her.

"Jeez, Simon, you nearly scared me half to—"

She stopped and studied him – he had on blue pyjamas and his feet were bare. His black hair stood up at odd angles, and he didn't look like a computer genius right then. No, he looked like a fire truck.

"Did you get some sun, Simon?" she asked.

Simon nodded. "Don't ever set up an observation post on a water tower."

"OK," Kat said softly. She wanted to reach out and pat his back, but she didn't know how far the burn went, and – more than that – she couldn't quite forget that she was the one who needed comforting.

"Where's Uncle Eddie?" Kat heard her voice break. She sounded and felt like a little girl when she told him, "I need Uncle Eddie."

"He's gone," Simon said. "Left a couple of hours ago. Uncle Felix was trying to run a Groundhog *with* a Black-eyed Susan and...well..."

"Gas lines?" Kat guessed.

Simon nodded. "Gas lines. Eddie left for Paraguay as soon as he heard." He glanced up and down the empty hall. "Where's Hale?"

There was an emptiness in Kat's gut, a dizzy feeling in the back of her mind. Uncle Eddie had left. Hale was gone. Constance Miller – whoever she really was – was a whole different type of missing, and suddenly, Kat couldn't take it. She had to do something, find something, be something other than the mark, so she pushed past Simon and into the office that she had seen used once or maybe twice in her entire life.

There was only one small window in that tiny room, and the light from the street barely broke through the heavy blinds, so Kat reached for the switch. Filing cabinets lined one side, topped with boxes and old envelopes, half-finished crossword puzzles and magazines from decades long since past. Behind the desk sat a wall of bookshelves filled with papers and tools, and dusty maps of the sewer system under the Louvre.

"What are you doing?" Simon asked while Kat pulled open the top drawer of the filing cabinet closest to the door. The drawer was rusty and squeaked, but Uncle Eddie was a continent away, so she pulled harder, pushed through the files faster.

A shoe box full of old IDs.

Blueprints for a very large bank written almost entirely in Japanese.

Background information on every guard at the Tower of London in 1980.

"Do you know if Uncle Eddie keeps anything about the other families?" She slammed the top drawer shut and jerked open the next.

Shipping manifests for a tanker out of Stockholm.

"What about them?" Simon asked.

Blank letterhead from the ambassador to Ecuador.

"Names? Addresses? Any information about the other families – how to track them down."

A ring of keys labelled Property of Montreal World's Fair, DO NOT DUPLICATE.

"I don't know," Simon said. He sounded almost afraid, standing there, watching Kat slam the second drawer then step back and look at the piles and the boxes and the dust. Looking for answers.

"Simon, I need you to tell me if Uncle Eddie keeps a computer anywhere. Have you ever built him any databases or an address book or—"

"Kat." Simon cut her off. "This is Uncle Eddie you're talking about."

She pulled the chair out from behind the desk, pushed aside a perfectly-to-scale model of the Egyptian Museum in Cairo, and took a seat.

"Kat, what is going on?" Simon said in the manner of a boy who had given up on trying to understand anything that wasn't made of ones and zeros. "What are you looking for?" Kat pulled open a desk drawer and ran her fingers through a million dollars in fake chips from a hotel that had never existed in Las Vegas. "What's wrong?" he asked as she thumbed through a book about the catacombs and passageways that still ran beneath Vatican City.

"Kat!" Simon yelled this time. He pulled the book out of her frantic hands. "Kat, where is Hale?"

And suddenly Kat knew she couldn't hide. Couldn't run. Couldn't lie.

"Hale is..." she started slowly.

"I'm right here."

And there he was, standing in the hallway at Simon's back. When Gabrielle appeared at his side, Kat didn't know what she was feeling: relief or embarrassment. Shame or guilt.

She tried to smile. "I thought you were heading to Paraguay."

He dropped the duffel bag to the ground and leaned against the door frame. "Yeah, but then I saw the most interesting thing on the news."

There was only one chair in the dusty office, little light, no food, but those weren't the reasons why they left. The kitchen was simply where these things were discussed, so the kitchen was where they went. Well, all of them but Katarina. Kat stayed by the door.

"So how was Paraguay?" Gabrielle asked as she and Hale and Simon took their places at the table.

"There were mosquitoes. I hate mosquitoes." Simon scratched at his leg, but his gaze drifted from Gabrielle to

Hale and finally to Kat. "What happened?"

Hale and Gabrielle looked at Kat. Kat looked away.

"We have a sort of...situation," Hale said.

To Hale's right, Simon winced. "Here," Gabrielle said, reaching for the burn cream Uncle Eddie kept over the stove. She grabbed the younger boy by the top of the head and said, "Hold still."

"Was it the Russians?" Simon asked. No one answered. "Brazil?" His voice was rising higher. "Don't tell me someone from the Henley finally—"

"It's Romani." Kat's voice cut him off. "Or...we thought it was Romani – I thought it was him. But then..."

"Kat." Hale was up and crossing the room. In a split second he reached her. "I believed them too."

"But I should know better."

"So it's OK if *I* get taken?"

She could tell she'd hurt him, and she hadn't even tried. "You wanted to leave, Hale. You tried to get *me* to leave."

"Um...can someone please tell me what happened?"

When Kat turned back to Simon, his face was oozing and covered with cream.

"We stole the Cleopatra Emerald," Gabrielle said simply, and Simon's face turned an even deeper shade of crimson.

"You stole the... *You* stole the... You *stole* the... How? Why? How?"

"Alice in Wonderland," Gabrielle said simply. "Kitty here swapped the real for a fake and zoomed right out of the rabbit hole without anyone suspecting a thing." She smiled at her cousin as if she were finally starting to approve. "It was beautiful."

"No." Kat shook her head. "It wasn't."

"But..." Simon's eyes were wide. His voice was cracking. "But Uncle Eddie says that the Cleopatra Emerald is—"

"It's not cursed," Hale said, but Kat couldn't shake the feeling that she wasn't so sure. *Cleopatra jobs always end badly.*

She fingered the card in her pocket and took her place at the table. "They said Romani sent them," Kat explained. "They said they were the stone's rightful owners and that Romani had sent them, and I..."

"What are you saying, Kat?"

She laughed at the joke that wasn't funny at all. And then Katarina Bishop, teen wonder thief and criminal It Girl finally told them, "I got conned."

The world didn't end when she said it. Kat had been expecting the brownstone's walls to crumble, the old kitchen table to crack in two beneath her palms. But what followed was nothing but an eerie, empty quiet, and Kat knew the girl she'd been two hours before was dead.

"So what?" Hale said after what felt like an eternity. "So we messed up. We learned. And it's over."

"No." Kat stood and put Romani's card on the table. She saw the three of them stare down at it, felt something in the room shift, the kitchen come alive as she whispered, "It's only just beginning."

FOURTEEN

It took almost an hour for Hale and Gabrielle to tell Simon the full story, and when they were finished, Kat didn't allow herself to think of all the things she did not know. She kept her mind centred, focused, trained on the thing that mattered most.

"How many people know the name Romani?"

"You mean besides everyone who heard about the random mystery man who broke into the Henley last autumn and left his calling card? Twice?" Simon asked.

"Yeah. How many people know Romani is a Chelovek Pseudonima – one of the sacred names?"

Hale backed away from the table, knowing he was out of his range, his depth, leaving the kids who had been borne into Uncle Eddie's kitchen to ponder.

"Twenty?" Gabrielle guessed. "Fifty?"

But Simon was shaking his head. "There's no way to know."

"Uncle Eddie would know," Kat murmured.

"No," Hale snapped. "Don't even think about telling

Uncle Eddie about this. Not yet. No." He shook his head as if changing his mind. "Not ever."

"This is Uncle Eddie's world, Hale. We've got to tell him. He's the only person who can help us," Kat said.

"There's got to be some other way. Look at me." Hale's eyes were warm and soft and comforting. He couldn't have been further from the boy in the limo when he told her, "We will find some other way."

"Are you *sure* you guys have never seen this woman before?" Simon asked, trying to process all the facts.

"I don't know..." Kat started slowly. "There was something about her that was...*familiar*. Did you feel it?"

Hale shook his head. "No."

"I thought that maybe I'd just seen her on the news – the real woman. But now..." Kat trailed off, totally unsure how anything was supposed to end.

"Simon, are you making a spreadsheet?" Gabrielle asked, spinning the laptop around on the table.

"Spreadsheets can be very beneficial," he said, spinning the laptop back.

"We need to ask Uncle Eddie," Kat said. "We've got to tell him – plead for forgiveness and beg for help."

She was standing, reaching for the old rotary-dial phone that hung on the kitchen wall, its long spiral cord dangling all the way to the floor. But Hale was flying across the room, his hands covering hers as, together, they gripped the receiver.

"Need to make a call?" she asked.

"I'm not going to let you do this, Kat," Hale said slowly.

"I'm not going to let you fall on some sword because you made a mistake. If you call down there—"

"What? I hear South America is lovely this time of year."

"Except for the mosquitoes," Simon added.

Kat nodded. "Except for the mosquitoes. It's as good a place as any to die."

Hale shook his head. "He'll never forgive you. Or you'll never forgive yourself. Either way, you'll lose him. Trust me. I know a little something about being the family disappointment." He gently pulled the receiver from Kat's hands. "Besides, everyone knows I blister when I burn."

"I don't recommend that either," Simon said while Gabrielle applied another dab of lotion.

Hale's voice was lower, the words meant only for Kat as he leaned closer, whispering, "Do you really think Uncle Eddie is going to forget that we stole the one thing he's ever forbidden anyone from stealing? How do you think he'll react when he finds out we used Charlie to help us? Trust me, Kat. I realise I haven't known him as long as you have, but if you tell Uncle Eddie about this—"

"What? He'll write me out of his will?"

"And you're gonna need a will." It might have been easy to forget Gabrielle was there, she was so quiet as she treated Simon, seemingly oblivious to it all. But when she stood and looked her cousin in the eye, there was no forgetting that Kat wasn't Uncle Eddie's only blood relative in the room. "Hale is right."

"But—" Kat started.

"But nothing. You wanna confess your sins to Uncle Eddie, fine. But you don't get to confess ours. And believe me, he won't just be angry, Kat." Gabrielle drew a breath. Her voice cracked. "He'll be *heartbroken*."

Hale leaned forward, pressing Kat against the wall, his arm reaching over her to slowly place the receiver back into its cradle.

"Romani *is* running this one, Kat," Hale said, his voice low and soft. "He wasn't at first, but he put that card in your pocket, so he's running things now. And now..." Kat actually felt the rise and fall of his chest when he took a deep breath. "And now we get the Cleopatra back."

"That is a great plan, guys. Really, it is," Kat said. "Except we can't steal what we can't find, and Uncle Eddie is the only person on earth who might know who these people are."

"The only person?" Gabrielle crossed her long legs and examined her nails. It sounded like the most innocent suggestion in the world when she said, "You're the genius, Kat. Surely you can think of *someone*."

ONE DAY AFTER
KAT MESSED UP

LYON,
FRANCE

FIFTEEN

It took approximately eighteen hours for Kat to form a plan and Hale to summon the jet, and for the four teens to find themselves standing on the streets of Lyon, France.

When the sun began to set in the distance, Kat stifled a yawn, but she knew she wasn't really sleepy. Tired people manage to sleep on private jets with very little difficulty or discomfort. Had it been mere exhaustion, Kat was certain she could have dozed in the chauffeured car that met them at the private airstrip just outside of town.

But as she walked among the vendors at the booming street markets, the colours seemed a little too bright, the noises a bit too loud. And when Hale held a warm croissant in her direction and said, "I'm buying," her reflexes were entirely too slow.

"Thanks," Gabrielle said, snatching the pastry from his hand and peeling away one long buttery strip.

So no, Kat realised, it wasn't just fatigue that plagued her reflexes and intuition. She had to entertain the notion that she was simply losing her touch.

Or maybe, Kat had to admit, she was just cursed.

Walking down the street that day, Lyon didn't seem like the second largest city in France. Farmers lined produce into stalls in the market. Shopkeepers swept their doorsteps, and two policemen walked quietly past four of the top thieves in the world, not even a little bit the wiser.

Gabrielle must not have shared Kat's newfound insomnia, because she yawned and stretched in the manner of someone who could get used to travelling in the style of W. W. Hale the Fifth.

Simon, on the other hand, didn't look like he would ever be comfortable again. "What time is your contact meeting us?"

"Oh, well, it's not really a meeting, strictly speaking," Kat told him.

Hale crossed his arms and leaned against the low stone wall that ran along the Rhône. "Strictly speaking, what is it?"

"It's more of a drop-by," Kat said.

"This contact doesn't know we're coming, does he?" Hale asked, but Kat turned away from his stare.

She was trying to decide how to answer when Gabrielle threw her hands into the air. "Great," she said. "He knows Uncle Eddie, doesn't he? He's going to talk to Uncle Eddie. You know, my mom expects me in Paraguay any day. And when I don't show—"

"No one's talking to Uncle Eddie, Gabs. Trust me."

"Just tell me this, Kat," Hale said, inching closer. "Is this mystery guy gonna know who our fake Constance was, or did we fly all the way to France for nothing?"

Kat could feel his impatience and his worry. The bored billionaire was gone, she knew. So was the hurt and worried boy who'd warned her about going too far. Constance – whoever she was – had taken more than just the Cleopatra when she'd told her lies and gone away.

"Look, guys," Kat said, taking the three of them in. "As far as I know, the world's best criminal database is inside of Uncle Eddie's head. Barring that, the second-best thing is here."

"Is this *thing* close?" Hale asked.

"Oh –" Kat took a deep breath – "you could say that."

There was a building on the other side of the river. Kat felt herself point, watched her friends turn and stare into the distance at the sun that reflected off the steel and the glass and the large sign that read *Interpol*.

"That's funny, Kat," Simon said, then realised that no one else was laughing. "No," he gasped, and Hale reached for Kat's arm.

"Let's chat."

Hale was taller, broader, stronger, but Kat could have stopped him if she'd wanted. Or at least that's what she told herself as he pulled her ten feet away from Simon and Gabrielle and spoke beneath his breath. "When you said you knew a source, I was thinking maybe...your dad," Hale confided.

"Constance, or whoever she is, is old school, Hale.

If Dad knew someone like that, trust me, I would have heard about her."

"Or if not your dad...then Charlie."

"I thought you didn't like Charlie."

"Charlie was weird. But weird is OK."

"I thought you were never driving up that mountain again if your life depended on it."

"There are helicopters. I'm good with helicopters."

"I thought you liked France."

Hale pointed across the river to the home of the world's police. "Some parts I like better than others!"

He pulled Kat gently towards him. "Someone else has got the information we need... There's got to be some other way."

"The other way is Uncle Eddie," Kat countered. "So, you tell me: which one is scarier?"

And with that, the four of them turned in perfect unison and stared at the gleaming building on the other side of the riverbank.

Gabrielle was the one who said what everyone else was thinking. "So when do we start?"

Even though Kat was sure the hotel suite was the biggest in Lyon (Marcus didn't know how to book any other kind), it still felt impossibly small seventy-two hours later as Hale paced and Gabrielle lounged and Simon's computers (if possible) multiplied.

"What time does it close?" Hale asked for what must have been the tenth time in the past two hours.

"It doesn't," Simon and Gabrielle said at the exact same time, then all three of them turned to glare at Kat.

"This –" Kat held out one hand – "or Uncle Eddie." She held out the other, balancing an imaginary scale

Simon shivered, then went on. "Well, like I was saying, since Interpol works – literally – all around the world, they are open twenty-four hours a day, always on in every time zone. So the place is never empty. And they've got cameras. Good ones."

"I should hope so." Gabrielle looked indignant. "I mean, they're Interpol, for crying out loud."

"They don't work with the public, so entry and exit is strictly controlled through these doors." Simon pointed to the main entrances on the screen.

"There is some good news, isn't there, Simon?" Gabrielle asked.

"From a security standpoint, their biggest concerns are terrorist attacks. Bombs. Hostage situations. They've got more biohazard detectors per square foot than any other building in Europe. Oh, and last year they spent about three million dollars on this facial recognition software that—"

"Good news," Hale reminded Simon with a pat on his back.

"They don't have anything anyone wants," Simon said, then he looked at Kat. "Well...normal people. No offence."

She shook her head. "None taken."

"It's really just an office building – cubicles and files and conference rooms. No cash. No art. Nothing to steal, so if you can get in, you can pretty much have the run of the place. I mean, aside from the guards."

"And the cameras," Gabrielle reminded him.

"And those. And they've got this biometric retinal scanner that keeps people out of places where they don't have clearance. But the rest is...easy. Even their computer system is impossible to hack from the outside, but once you're inside..."

"Then let's get inside," Kat said.

If there was one thing any member of Kat's family learned at an early age it was that fear is a weakness. It makes a person lose her nerve and her cool. It makes people jumpy and organisations nervous, and when that happens, there is always a chance to take advantage. So when Simon and Gabrielle looked at each other, Kat could see a single thought settling onto both of their faces.

"Florence Nightingale," they both said with a sigh.

"What?" Hale looked between them. Kat couldn't decide if he was more frustrated with himself or with her. But in any case, he looked very much like someone who would never get used to being on the outside of the joke. "What? So you expect us to just stroll into the headquarters of the International Criminal Police Organization? For them to throw open the doors and let us in?"

Kat smiled as she turned to him. "That's *exactly* what I expect to happen."

"Um..." Simon started slowly, "at the risk of stating the obvious, I feel I have to point out that Interpol has the world's best database of international criminals."

"That's the idea," Gabrielle said with a nod.

"And I feel compelled to remind you that *we're* international criminals?" he finished, but Kat was already smiling.

"Don't worry, Simon. It's not like anyone in there knows it was a bunch of teenagers who robbed the Henley."

8 DAYS AFTER
KAT GOT CONNED

LYON,
FRANCE

SIXTEEN

Amelia Bennett had not become the highest-ranking woman in Interpol's lowest-ranking department by not being able to read between lines or connect dots. Most people would see working at the world headquarters as a promotion – a step up. To the outside observer, Interpol's main office was the epitome of crime-solving for the twenty-first century, and yet to Amelia Bennett it was a like a prison.

But with a far more interesting basement.

Strolling through headquarters that Friday morning, she had a stack of dusty files under her arm and a look of steely resolve on her face, and when she reached her boss's door, she walked right in without knocking.

"Bennett!" Artie Dupree snapped. "What are you—" But the sound of fifteen pounds of dusty files and logbooks hitting the desk cut him off. "What is all this?"

"Evidence," Amelia said.

The man fingered one of the files in front of him. "The Turkish Dagger job? That happened in 1916, didn't it?"

Amelia crossed her arms and smiled. "Yes, it did."

Then it was her boss's turn to smirk. "Well, thank goodness you've solved it."

As a trained investigator and highly intuitive woman, Amelia heard the dismissal in her superior's voice, but she chose not to acknowledge it.

"He did it, Artie."

"Who?"

Amelia placed her palms on the desk and leaned towards him. "Visily Romani."

Artie huffed. "The Henley investigation is in the hands of the proper authorities, Amelia. Unless the basement archives have a secret passage to London that I know nothing of, I'd recommend—"

Amelia moved a hand to one trim hip and looked down at the man behind the desk. "I really have to thank you, Artie. I mean, do you know what you get when you spend eight weeks going through boxes of dead files?"

Artie craned his neck upwards in order to look at her. "Paper cuts?"

"History." Amelia smiled as if the joke, ultimately, were on him. She picked up the file closest and tossed it onto the end of the desk. "Vienna in 1962. Paris in 1926." Another file landed on top of the stack, and the man looked physically pained – as if that much dust and disorder were too much for his delicate senses.

"What do they have in common?" she asked like a professor challenging a student.

"Now see here, Amelia, I am a very busy—"

"All high-profile targets. All impeccably planned – almost elegant – jobs."

"Amelia, really..."

"And in every file you can find one name: *Visily Romani*." She rummaged through the files, pulling out flagged pieces of paper and showing them to her boss. "Shipping manifest from Berlin in 1935 –" she pointed to a signature – "Romani. Witness statement out of Turkey. The witness's name—"

"Romani," Artie Dupree finished for her, then gave an exasperated sigh. "What's this got to do with the Henley?"

"A dozen high-profile heists in a dozen cities over the course of the past ninety years. And who knows how long before that?"

And then it was her boss's turn to grin. "Ninety years?" he said, sounding as if he might be considering taking the bait. "Mr Romani has been a very busy man."

"But that's the thing, Artie. What if Romani isn't a man?" Amelia said, leaning forward.

"Great. We'll alert Scotland Yard and tell them they're looking for a vampire. Or a werewolf. I'm assuming you've cross-referenced this with the lunar cycles."

"What if it's a *name*?" Amelia said, undaunted. She spread the files across the desk. "A name that has been used by a lot of people for a very long time."

"Excellent." Her boss pushed the files aside and returned to his order and his lists and his life. "You cracked it. Great work. I'll call the Henley right away and tell them Leonardo's *Angel Returning to Heaven* was stolen by a name."

"These are some of the most famous unsolved crimes in history. Don't you see that?"

"I see that they're decades old, and the key word is *unsolved*."

"It's a common link. A thread. These crimes are interconnected, and if we—"

"Do you know where the *Angel* is?" he snapped, and Amelia gave an involuntary backwards step.

"No."

"Do you have information that will lead to the arrest of this Romani..." He stumbled, flustered. "Or Roman*is*?"

"If we launch an investigation..."

"Bennett! The last time we let you lead an investigation, you swore you would catch one Robert Bishop."

Amelia crossed her arms and stared down. "Yes, I can see how that investigation would be such a disappointment. It only resulted in the arrest of an international criminal and the recovery of a million-dollar statue and four priceless paintings that had been missing for sixty years."

"If you really want to solve what happened at the Henley, I'd suggest you talk to your son." Artie Dupree slipped on his glasses. "After all, he was there... Wait, *what was* he doing there, again?" The man asked the question that he and a few dozen others had already asked before.

"He told me he was there out of a deep love of art."

"But you don't believe him?"

"He's a teenage boy. I'm sure what he really meant to say was that he was there to impress some girl."

The man studied her as if this were all new information (it wasn't). He sighed as if he could completely understand her predicament (he couldn't). And he looked at her as if his smile could take the sting out of her current situation (it didn't even come close).

"Then I'm going to assume there's nothing else I can do for you, Agent Bennett?"

"No," Amelia said, gathering the dusty files and clutching them to her black suit. "I have quite everything I need."

Despite being a highly trained and deftly skilled observer, there were many things Amelia Bennett did not see on her trip back to the basement archives. After all, it looked like a typical morning with the sleepy-eyed masses swiping cards and coming inside. Workers pushed carts and people scanned papers, and it was a day just like any other, there on the banks of the Rhône.

Well, at least that was the way it seemed right up until the point when the bouquet of fresh flowers that was meant for the deputy director was carried from the main reception desk to the upper-level offices, setting off a half dozen biohazard detectors along the way.

A few moments later, on the second floor, a bottle of carpet cleaner began to bubble with seemingly toxic fumes. The head of Interpol's internal security division was halfway to the mailroom when he heard that a brand-new espresso machine had spontaneously caught on fire. A recently serviced oven in the cafeteria began spewing smoke so thick no one could even see.

"What's going on?" one of the guards in the security room wanted to know.

"All of the toilets in the men's room on the fourth floor just...blew!" someone else exclaimed.

All throughout the building, sirens were blaring and sensors were tripping. And when the electronic voice began echoing through the building, saying, "THERE HAS BEEN A BREACH IN SECURITY PROTOCOL. PLEASE PROCEED TO THE NEAREST DOOR," first in French, then again in Arabic, English and Spanish, there was only one thing to be done.

To their credit, every single person at Interpol's world headquarters reacted in the calm, orderly way that one would have expected. To anyone observing from across the river, it looked like nothing more than a minor inconvenience – a drill. Exploding toilets, after all, did not an international incident make. Many of the Interpol officials said later that if they hadn't known better, they would have sworn they were witnessing the harmless pranks of kids.

Well, at least that was the way it seemed until the fire trucks appeared with their swirling lights and screaming sirens. The police, too, were quick to the scene – almost too quick, some might say – to throw up the barricades and block off the traffic.

But it wasn't until they saw the big bus from the bomb squad that the people huddled on the pavements began to wonder if things might be more severe than some elaborate prank.

"Step aside!" the tallest of the masked figures in the heavy protective suits yelled. He barked orders at a man with a walkie-talkie. "Your people are out of there?"

"Yes," the man said. He looked vaguely confused and more than a little annoyed. "But it was just the toilets... Can't we go back inside and—"

"Now, you listen to me," the masked man yelled. He had a deep voice, and when he spoke, the whole crowd seemed to stop and listen. "This facility has the best bio-hazard detectors that money can buy, and in the past twenty minutes, nine of them have gone off. We take that sort of thing seriously in my department. What about you?"

The man with the walkie-talkie stayed quiet, weighing the image of rogue espresso machines and malfunctioning toilets against the words of the masked man. "Do what you have to do," he said, leaving the four masked figures to walk through Interpol's gleaming, polished doors.

Katarina Bishop was not claustrophobic, or so she told herself with every breath she took inside the heavy mask. She'd once flown from Cairo to Istanbul locked inside a solid-gold sarcophagus, after all, so it wasn't the tiny space that was causing Kat's heart to pound or her face to sweat as she followed Hale up the big sweeping staircase, rushing to the mainframe that was housed on the second floor.

Hale stopped at the top of the landing, looked in both directions, and pulled the mask from his head.

"Simon, you're down there." He pointed to the long

empty hall. "Gabrielle, you can—"

But then Hale couldn't finish. Kat couldn't move. None of them could do anything but watch when Gabrielle's foot caught on the top step, and her ankle turned, and Gabrielle went falling, tumbling down the stairs, onto the landing below.

Kat and Simon looked at each other as if to verify that they had seen the same thing – that Gabrielle...had fallen.

Only Hale managed to rush toward her. "Are you OK?"

But even Gabrielle herself couldn't seem to process what had happened. She looked up and found her cousin's eyes. "Kat, did I just...fall?"

"Yeah," Kat said. "I think you did."

"But I never fall," Gabrielle countered, as if there had to be some kind of mistake.

"Can you stand on it?" Hale asked, reaching for her, but Gabrielle just laughed.

"Of course I can— Ow!" The pain that flashed across her face was quick and intense, but it was a different kind of panic that bled through her voice when she said, "Kat, I can't stand."

"I know, Gabs. It'll be OK. Just sit here on the steps and wait for us. Simon and Hale can take the mainframe. I'll check the hard files in the archives and—"

"I'm cursed," Gabrielle said, as if she hadn't heard a word. "I sent the Cleopatra Emerald skidding across the floor and now I'm...cursed."

"Don't be silly," Kat said, reaching for her cousin.

"Don't touch me!" Gabrielle said. "It might be contagious."

"Kat..." There was a tenor of impatience and fear in Hale's voice. "We gotta move," he said, and he was right.

"Go," Gabrielle snapped. "I can keep an eye on the doors from here."

"But..." Simon started.

"Go!" Gabrielle yelled, and Kat knew what had to be done.

"How long until the real bomb squad shows up?" Hale asked, risking a glance out the massive windows.

"Best-case scenario?" Kat asked. Hale nodded. "Hurry."

So Kat was alone as she made her way into the depths of the building, past the division of counterterrorism intelligence, through an entire corridor marked with the portraits of past secretaries-general. It should have been the ultimate in trespassing – walking through those particular halls. But it felt like just another office building, and she ran faster, relying on the blueprints in her mind to lead her to the small door with the even smaller sign that read ARCHIVES.

She pushed her way inside, hurtling down the stairs, deeper and deeper into the belly of the building.

"Simon, what's your status?" she heard Gabrielle ask from three floors away.

"Well, their encryption is really good, but I've managed to launch a worm into their—"

"English, buddy," Hale reminded him.

"Almost there."

"Kat?" Hale asked just as Kat reached the bottom of the staircase and pushed open another door. She stepped onto a small landing. "Kat?" He asked again. "What's your—"

"Uh...guys..." Kat gripped the cold pipe rail. "You know how Interpol's sort of a clearinghouse for information?" She didn't wait for an answer. "I think I just found...the house."

From her place on the landing at the top of the stairs, Kat could easily see the room that stretched out before her, as vast and endless as a maze. Shelves and filing cabinets – thousands of filing cabinets – filled the space that seemed as long as the building itself. Dim industrial lights hung overhead, and the whole place smelled of dust and disuse. Looking down, Kat couldn't shake the feeling that what she'd really found was the graveyard – the place where old jobs go after they die.

"Twenty-five per cent downloaded," Simon said from above.

Kat bounded down the stairs, following the faded signs through dusty aisles that felt lightyears away from the sleek offices and modern fixtures that dominated the floors above. She ran until she finally reached the deepest, darkest part of the room and the cabinets dedicated to art and cultural crimes.

"Hey...guys..." Kat heard Gabrielle say. "What will the *real* bomb squad look like?"

"Us," Kat heard herself say at the same time as Simon and Hale.

"Then it might be time to start heading for the exits," Gabrielle warned, and Kat felt her heart beat faster.

"OK, I got it. I'm good," Simon exclaimed.

"Gabrielle, I'm coming to get you," Hale said.

Kat could practically feel her crew working, acting, moving towards the exits in an orderly fashion, but she felt lost among the dozens of filing cabinets standing before her. It was like staring at a slightly less organised, highly abbreviated version of Uncle Eddie's mind.

"Kat." Hale's voice was steady and even in her ear. "No crazy chances," he warned.

"No crazy chances," Kat said, and started throwing open drawers. She didn't know what she was looking for, but she moved like lightning, scouring files for any mention of jewel heists, con artists, or particularly conniving older women who might know enough to call upon the name Romani.

"OK," Gabrielle said, "it looks like the security head is fighting with the bomb guys. We've got to go."

"Already on my way," Hale said, and Kat slammed another drawer.

She turned, her gaze sweeping along the filing cabinets to her right, then sliding across the tall metal shelves on her left. She stood there, knowing she could never search it all, fearing the truth might be there, rotting away with the rest of the dead files.

And that was when she saw it – a file box on a dusty shelf just above her head. There was an old photo taped to the label. The picture itself was black-and-white – no colour of any kind – but Kat knew the stone in the picture was a vivid, vibrant green. She knew because just a week before she'd held it in her hand.

"Kat!" Hale's voice echoed through her ear.

"Coming!" Kat yelled, and pulled the box from the shelf. She was already racing back through the stacks and rows when her phone began to ring, the sound as loud as a siren in the massive echoing space.

She dropped the heavy box onto a small wooden table and began rifling through the pockets of her bomb squad suit, looking for the phone. But it had stopped ringing, and suddenly Kat found herself looking down at a mountain of old logbooks and dusty folders. On top of it all lay a yellow legal pad, hasty scribbles covering the page. Arrows pointed from every corner, linking every thought to a single name.

Romani.

"Kat, we're almost to the rendezvous point. I don't see you." Hale's voice echoed in her ear, but the pile of folders kept pulling her closer.

"Kat!" Hale snapped, but the files were right there, full of secrets that only a handful of people in the world had ever known.

They were right there.

She could wait. She could look. She could—

"Kat," Hale said again, "are you coming?"

"Just one minute."

"I don't think we have a minute," Hale said just as, three floors away, the sirens began to wail. The basement lights flickered. And Kat knew she had no choice but to turn away from the table and say, "I'll be there soon."

She'd just picked up the box and started to run when something made her stop dead in her tracks.

"I know, sir," a voice said behind Kat, hidden deep within the maze of shelves. "Well, the alarms don't sound in the subbasement, do they? I'm sorry, I must have missed them." There was a long pause with nothing but the sound of high heels on the concrete floor.

That voice, Kat thought. Those heels. She looked at the worktable once again, the careful circles and pile of files all bearing the name Romani, and Kat knew exactly who was heading her way.

"Yes," Amelia said. "Of course I'm going to the emergency exit right now," she lied. Kat heard the woman turn the corner through the stacks, so she shoved the box under a nearby desk and followed it, realising too late that someone else was already under the table.

"Kat?" an all-too familiar voice said. "Is that you?"

Kat felt her phone vibrate, and she jerked it from her pocket before it could ring again, cursing her own carelessness and...well...curses.

"Kat, are you there?" her father echoed over the phone.

But Kat...Kat sat staring into the eyes she hadn't seen in months and said, "Dad, I better call you back."

In the thief's lexicon, there are many different words for *busted. Made. Blown.* They all applied right then, of course, but those were not the words that came to Kat's mind.

"Nick?" she asked, her voice barely a whisper. "What are you doing—"

"Shh." He pulled her tightly to him, and in the silence,

Kat heard the woman walking closer.

"So..." Kat whispered when the woman had turned down another aisle, "your mom got transferred. I guess finding four priceless paintings and getting an international criminal off the streets does wonders for a woman's career."

"Not as much as having your son locked in a room at the Henley will do."

Kat shrugged. "Sorry about that."

"No problem." Nick glanced from Kat to the dusty file box with the big green stone on its label. "Doing some research?"

"Article for the high school paper. You?"

"Take Your Son to Work Day." His lie was just as quick and almost as easy as her own.

"Kat!" Hale was screaming in her ear. "Kat, where are you? I'm coming back in to get you."

"No," Kat said, and the look in Nick's eyes told her that he knew exactly what she was thinking.

"Time to go?" he asked.

"Yeah," Kat said, pushing the box out from underneath the desk and starting to follow. But just then, Nick reached out and held her arm.

"Where are you going?"

"Away," Kat said, as if the answer should be obvious.

"Don't use the main stairs," he warned, then pointed to a dark corner in the distance. "There's an emergency exit back there. I think someone disabled the sensors and rigged the lock this morning."

"Oh, *someone* did?" she asked.

Nick nodded, crawled from under the desk, and turned in the direction his mother was heading.

"Nick?" Kat risked the extra second and the noise. She lifted the box. "What file were you looking for?"

He shrugged. "Yours."

SEVENTEEN

It was relatively easy to get to the plane. Customs was no problem. What was difficult, Kat realised, was staring through the windows of the New York-bound private jet and seeing for the first time that the world was a totally different place from what you had ever thought it to be.

"What about her?" Simon asked. He'd taped a white sheet to the bulkhead at the front of the cabin, and Kat turned back to it, looked at the image on the makeshift screen of a gorgeous woman dressed exactly like the Crown Princess Anastasia. "Of course, this was taken fifty years ago, but—"

"No," Kat said, and shook her head.

"Her?" Simon asked, and the image changed to a young woman in a sarong, riding an elephant.

Another "No", this time from Hale.

"What about *her*?"

"That's Uncle Felix in drag, Simon," Kat told him.

"*Oh, yeah*," Simon and Hale said, tilting their heads and staring at a surprisingly striking figure in an equally striking hat at the royal wedding of Charles and Diana.

Hale was systematically shifting through the mound of files that Kat had carried from Interpol's basement. Simon had his computers and wires and screens, and soon data from Interpol began flashing through the cabin at 32,000 feet.

Kat herself was left to stare out of the window at the tiny towns and green countryside that eventually gave way to deep blue ocean, thinking that it wasn't such a small world after all. Sure, it was an odd thing to realise for the first time at the age of fifteen, but the brownstone's kitchen was no more than a twelve-by-twelve room... With the exception of three short months the previous fall, Kat had never known a world where everyone didn't know her father and hadn't loved her mother, where Eddie wasn't "Uncle" to every soul she knew.

So Kat stared out at the vastness and whispered, "The world –" she reached to touch the glass – "is *big*."

"And cursed," Gabrielle added, manoeuvring her bruised body awkwardly into the plush leather chair across from Kat's. She plopped her swollen ankle onto her cousin's lap. "So, Katarina, back at Interpol...you were late."

Even the best cons eventually meet someone to whom they cannot lie, and like it or not, Kat realised, for her that person was Gabrielle. In the deep silence that passed between them, both cousins seemed to know it.

"Got delayed," Kat answered.

"I see."

"It's not a big deal," Kat tried.

"I'm sure it's not."

"There was a hitch." Kat shrugged.

"There always is." Gabrielle leaned closer and whispered, "Just tell me, does this hitch have a name?"

Kat started to answer, but just then her cousin's eyes went wide, and Kat knew, without looking, that Hale was standing behind her. She felt his hands settle on her shoulders as he leaned over the seat.

"Hey."

She looked up at him. "Hey."

"You OK?" he asked, taking the seat beside her. He felt big and warm and safe and...terrifying. Yeah, terrifying was definitely the right word, because he leaned close to examine Gabrielle's ankle, and all Kat could do was think, *I kissed you. I kissed you. I kissed you!*

"Kat?" Hale asked again.

"I'm fine," she said, a little too quickly.

Hale looked at Gabrielle, who crossed her arms, stared at her cousin, and said, "OK. Now the real answer."

"Nothing. It's just that..." Kat shook her head and turned back to the window. "The world is big."

In the reflection of the glass she saw Hale. He reminded her of her father, full of charm and hope. "Not *so* big, right?" he said. "There are...what? Six major families?"

"Seven," Kat and Gabrielle answered together.

Hale pointed to one of Simon's computers. "But this says six."

"The Australians sort of split in the eighties."

"Nasty business." Gabrielle shivered. "Never get between

two brothers and a sunken ship from the Spanish Armada. Trust me."

"OK, good." Hale stood and strolled to where Simon sat with his computers. "Seven families. That's a start. What else do we have?"

"Well," Gabrielle said with a sigh, "we know she was smart enough to find Kat and play her – no offence."

"None taken," Kat said.

"And…" Gabrielle spoke slowly, emphasising every word, "*she's a woman.*"

"Very good, Gabrielle," Hale tried to mock, but then he read the expression on Kat's face. "What?"

"How many girls do you know in this business?" she asked him.

"Well…I know you two…" He trailed off, utterly stumped.

"Exactly. It's a boys' club, big guy." Gabrielle crossed her good leg over the other as if to say she wouldn't have it any other way. "There can't be that many women who—"

Simon looked up from his keyboard. "According to Interpol, there are nine hundred and seventy-six." He pointed to the images on the screen that were flashing through at regular intervals. "These are just the ones they have pictures for – which isn't saying much. Most are just names – a lot are probably aliases. It would help if we had an age."

"Fifty?" Hale guessed at the exact time Kat said, "Eighty?"

"Or a *range*…" Simon said, putting the data into the computer. "What about a nationality?"

"She used a British accent, but…" Hale started.

"She could be *from* anywhere," Kat went on. "She could be on her way *to* anywhere. Let's face it, guys –" Kat shook her head – "this woman could be anyone."

"Not anyone," Hale said. "I mean, I'm fairly certain she isn't my aunt Myrtle."

Kat felt her hopes falling. "And even if we know who she is – it doesn't give us a clue *where* she is or why she...and her *grandson*...did it."

Hale laughed. "Even on the black market, the emerald's got to be worth millions of dollars, Kat. That's plenty of reason right there."

"But why do it this way?" Kat had to ask. "Why risk the wrath of Eddie and tick off an entire family if you can help it?"

"Easy." Hale sat down and kicked his feet up. "They couldn't help it."

"But...why?" Kat asked. It felt good to fixate on the question, the puzzle. "Why risk having us do their dirty work when anybody who'd know the name Romani would also know half a dozen crews just as good? This woman..." Kat trailed off, words failing, as if she couldn't even trust herself to speak.

"What?" Gabrielle asked, inching closer.

"It was nothing. Just...for a second I thought–"

"You knew her?" Gabrielle guessed.

Kat thought about the moment in the park – the look in the woman's eyes when she'd called to Kat and said thank you.

"No. It was more like *she* knew *me*. Like she was appraising me and the job. Like she knew better than some little old lady from Loxley, and so *I* should have known better." Kat felt herself trying to find the right words. "She looked at me like Uncle Eddie looks at me."

"*The female Uncle Eddie.*" Gabrielle's voice was full of awe and fear in equal measure, like the woman was a cross between a dragon and a unicorn – just as mythical and twice as deadly.

There was a TV on in the background, and the anchors talked of moving weather fronts and falling stock prices, as if those were the things in the world that really mattered.

"Uh...guys," Simon said, but Kat had turned back to the window.

"Why con us into stealing the Cleopatra Emerald?" she said quietly, repeating the question that was sending them across the ocean and back again. It was the question, Kat knew, that could haunt her for the rest of her life.

"Guys..." Simon said again, voice rising, but Kat was lost in thought, staring at the glass.

"Why con us?" she whispered.

"Maybe because of..." Simon seemed to lose his voice before choking out, "That?"

Kat spun back in time to see him raise a finger and point at the TV and the picture of the woman that Kat had come to know as Constance Miller. For a second, she thought Simon had found her somewhere among Interpol's files – until she realised the picture was live, and the woman was standing under the glare of what seemed like a thousand flashing bulbs, holding the Cleopatra Emerald out for all to see.

Simon cleared his throat. "OK, is it just me, or does this make her the worst thief ever?"

EIGHTEEN

Although the plane was state of the art, the pilots perfectly trained, Kat couldn't shake the feeling that they were falling, plummeting out of the sky. That was the only thing that could explain the knot in her stomach as Simon turned up the volume on the TV and she read the words at the bottom of the screen. *Live News Conference: Monaco.*

"Did they find the fake?" Hale said, leaning closer to the screen. "Is it an arrest?"

"No." Kat's voice was flat and even, as if she were watching it all from outside her body. She had the kind of distance – the perspective – that would make even her great-uncle proud. "*It's a con.*"

Together they watched as a balding man in a nice suit stepped behind the podium. "*Mesdames et messieurs,* members of the press, I am Pierre LaFont of the LaFont Auction House here in Monaco. On behalf of Mrs Brooks and myself, I thank you for coming today."

He spoke English with a heavy French accent. He didn't look up again until he'd finished.

"I will read a brief statement and then Mrs Brooks has agreed to take questions." He slipped on a pair of bifocals and studied a piece of paper, but the room stayed silent, transfixed.

"Three days ago, Mrs Margaret Brooks was examining a collection of antiques procured by her late husband and recently shipped to her winter home near Nice, France. One of the pieces – an urn – broke in transit. It was then that Mrs Brooks found a large emerald that presumably had been hidden inside. The stone is ninety-seven carats and of the highest quality. A team of experts is now en route to Monaco, where detailed appraisals, examinations and verifications will take place. In the meantime, it is my expert opinion that – due to the size, quality, and cut of the emerald in question – what Mrs Margaret Brooks has found is most likely the Antony Emerald."

The man took a deep breath, as if he'd just dived off a cliff. "And now Mrs Brooks will take questions."

If the members of the press looked dumbfounded, their reaction was nothing compared to that of the four teenagers who sat watching it all unfold from thirty thousand feet. On the other side of the cabin, Simon's slide show was still playing. Photos of every con woman that Interpol had ever known were flashing through the cabin, but none of them could hold a candle to the woman on the television then.

The matronly clothes and wig were gone, and when the woman spoke, her accent was big and brash and Southern.

"First, don't be like Pierre here. Y'all call me Maggie."

"Maggie! Maggie!" the reporters yelled, vying for her attention.

"Well, y'all sure are going to a lot of fuss for one little ol' rock." She scanned the crowd, savouring the spotlight, before settling on one especially handsome international correspondent. "Sweetheart, what I can do for you?"

The entire crowd laughed as if on cue.

The man smirked. "Do you believe in the curse, Maggie?"

Again, Maggie eyed the younger man up and down. "Maybe I believe in fate. What's your name, cutie?" she asked, but didn't really wait for an answer. "Folks," she said instead, leaning closer to the crowd and growing serious. "I'm from Texas. I've been hunting, shooting and riding since I could walk. I've married and buried four men, each richer than the last – God rest their souls," she added quickly, almost as if from habit. "So one little ol' rock doesn't scare me."

"Why not keep it, Maggie?" another reporter yelled.

"I'm rich," she snapped. "And I'm old. Now, they tell me that emerald can't make me younger, but it *can* make me richer. So one week from today, I'm gonna sell this thing to the highest bidder. And I'm betting someone's gonna bid pretty high." She made a move as if to leave.

"The Cold Shoulder," Kat and Hale said together. It was a classic move. Simple. And very, very effective because the crowd yelled louder, "Maggie!"

"Yes." She stopped and looked at them as if they were

little kids and she couldn't quite believe they hadn't run away to play.

"How did it feel knowing your movers had broken a two-thousand-year-old urn?" yelled a reporter near the back of the crowd.

This time it was Maggie's turn to laugh. "Like maybe I ought to let 'em break everything I own!"

"Do you think the emerald's real?" one of the reporters yelled.

"Well, I didn't imagine it."

When the crowd chuckled again, Kat recognised the sound. It was the laugh of the mark – the sign that they adored you, they believed you, and they would hand you their grand-mother's pearls, the key to the vault. Anything. Everything. Because right then, they...were in love.

Maggie's Southern accent might have been a fake (then again, maybe it wasn't), but she was the belle of the ball and not a soul would dare deny it.

"Let 'em run their little tests, boys. I think we all know what they're gonna find."

Even after the press conference was over, the four teens sat perfectly still for a long time, trying to understand what they'd just seen.

"People think she's going to sell the Antony," Gabrielle said, her voice a mixture of dismay and admiration.

"In seven days," Simon added.

"In Monaco," Kat said, turning her gaze to Hale, both of them knowing exactly what they had to do.

"Marcus," Hale said, pressing a button and calling to the cockpit. "We're gonna need to turn the plane around."

6 DAYS BEFORE
THE AUCTION

MONTE CARLO,
MONACO

NINETEEN

The fact that no one had ever heard of Margaret Covington Godfrey Brooks before then was something that, in the days that followed, was never mentioned.

The matriarchs of Atlanta suddenly recalled lunching with her during the years when she and her late second husband had supposedly kept a home in Buckhead. The alumni board of Texas A&M University was not surprised to find a backlog of cancelled cheques and generous donations even though, until then, the name had not been familiar to a single soul beyond its appearance on an old student register dating back to the 1950s. The residents of East Hampton seemed to recall a series of grand parties on Maggie's third husband's summer estate. And at least two former US presidents were rumoured to have been hunting buddies with Maggie herself on eighty thousand acres in the panhandle east of Lubbock (they also said that Maggie was the best shot any of their party had ever seen).

These weren't lies, Kat knew. They were merely the fruits of the seeds that only a great con artist could have planted and an all-powerful con could have grown.

Within twenty-four hours after the news of the Antony's recovery, Maggie's name and photo had been beamed around the world, and so it stood to reason that the woman who had not, technically, existed a mere week before had become a personality of international proportions.

Celebrity, after all, is nothing but a matter of perception.

And perception, Kat knew, was the true heart of the con.

So no one thought to verify the name or the bank accounts or any of the facts that appeared along with the woman with the emerald.

Because when there's a ninety-seven-carat emerald involved, the woman holding it is easily lost in the spotlight.

Even a woman like Maggie.

"There she is."

Only hours before, Kat had started to fear that the woman on the other side of the street was a figment of her imagination – a nightmare, a ghost. Of course, technically, Margaret Brooks *didn't* exist, but Kat had only to watch the woman, hear her big brass voice, and know that she was no phantom. Kat thought of what Constance...or Maggie...had dared to do, and a part of her couldn't help but think that Maggie... was legend.

She certainly couldn't ignore the irony that after chasing Maggie halfway around the world, fearing that she had disappeared like smoke, they had found her within twenty minutes of landing at the small private airstrip just outside of Nice.

Of course, it helped that the country of Monaco was no larger than a village, less than one square mile of rocky coastlines and pricey hotels. But the real reason they had found her so easily, Kat had to admit, was that Maggie was making absolutely no effort to hide.

Photographers snapped and passers-by shouted, and Maggie waved to them all with gusto as she walked from elegant shop to elegant shop, dining at the best restaurants, taking tea with only the best people.

Kat hated her. And Kat envied her. But mostly, she tried to imagine what it would be like to *be* her – to be that good, that smart, that sure. Thief years were like dog years, her father had always said, so by that count, Kat felt much older than fifteen; but standing on the street that night, staring through the windows of the five-star hotel that Maggie was temporarily calling home, Kat couldn't help feeling naive and inexperienced and...young. And she didn't exactly like it.

When her phone began to ring and she looked down to see it was her father calling, she felt young for entirely different reasons.

"You're going to have to talk to him eventually, you know."

She turned to see Hale standing behind her, jacket thrown over his shoulder, looking like he'd just stepped out of a movie.

Kat took one last glance at the phone, then slipped it back into her pocket. "As soon as he hears my voice, he'll know something's wrong."

"And that's a bad thing because..."

"He can't do this for me, Hale. This is my mess. I've got to clean it up." The sun had set, and as they walked towards the beach, Kat could see the moon rising over the Mediterranean. It was quiet there. Still and peaceful, as good a place as any to say, "And that's why I've been thinking...you should go."

Kat stopped suddenly. She felt Hale almost slam into her, saw the way Gabrielle and Simon watched from five feet away. Everyone was looking. Everyone was waiting. She felt like the most conspicuous thief in the world when she told the boy beside her, "You were right, Hale. It was a bad job. It was a bad call. You were right to leave."

"Kat..." Hale tried to reach for her, but even in the sand, Kat was quick and sure on her feet, and she moved nimbly away, leaving Hale with nothing but a fistful of salty air.

"Thanks for coming back and helping me find her and all, but..." She looked at Gabrielle, who stood leaning against Simon, still bruised and almost broken. "I think I've got to take it from here."

Kat didn't know where the stone was or how to steal it. She didn't know if she could best Maggie or how. All she knew for certain was that no one else was getting hurt because of her. She was sure right up until the point when Hale said, "No."

"What?" Kat said, spinning on him.

"I said no."

"What do you think's going to happen when you and

Simon and Gabrielle don't show up in Uruguay?"

"Paraguay," the three of them corrected in unison.

"The whole family's supposed to be there." She turned to Simon. "Do you think your dad won't notice when you don't come back?" She looked at her cousin. "You think your mom and Uncle Eddie won't send out a search party looking for you?"

The three of them stood silent, suddenly unable to answer, so Kat smiled at Hale and Gabrielle. "Both of you knew stealing the Cleopatra was a bad call, so it wasn't your mistake. Simon, you weren't even in the country, which means this isn't your problem. None of you. So you should all go. You can cover for me and—"

"No," Hale said again, just as flat and twice as certain.

"You don't get it, Hale. They're not gonna leave the Antony Emerald just lying around – even if it isn't the real one."

"And we're really only good at the 'lying around' jobs," he countered.

"She's already got the auction set. The clock is ticking."

Hale inched closer. "Timing is everything."

"Yeah." Kat looked up at him, eyes wide. "It is! And..." The words were gone, her mind suddenly blank, and Kat realised that she could no longer think, much less plan or theorise, plot or scheme. "And I'm not leading you guys into almost certain chaos." She shook her head. "Not again."

Hale shrugged. "I for one like chaos. Chaos looks good to me."

"You should get away from me. You should save yourselves

before I make you pass out or catch the measles or spontaneously combust or something." She looked at Hale for a long time, then shook her head. "I can't make you do this. Any of you. I can't—"

"Hey!" Hale crossed the small space between them in a flash. "No one *makes* me do anything. Not my family. Not your family...not even you."

"That's not what I meant."

"If I wanted to go, I'd go. But if I'm here, then *I'm here*. All of me." Kat felt his free hand brush her hair away from her face. "So what's it gonna be, Kat?"

It's a great curse of the con that you can look at anything and see a dozen angles. There are always loopholes, wormholes, cracks that you can slip through if only you know how to see them. And Kat was the kind of girl who *had* to see them. But right then, with Hale so close and the moon so bright, her mind was filled with nothing but fog.

"I think better when I'm alone, Hale. *I'm* better alone."

"No." Hale shook his head. "You really aren't."

"No one else is going to get hurt because of me!" Kat gave an involuntary glance at Gabrielle, who hobbled forward.

"You think sending me away is going to keep me from getting hurt?" her cousin asked. "Ha! I'm cursed, Kitty Kat. And the way I see it, my best bet at getting *uncursed* is to put that rock back where it belongs. So, sorry. You're stuck with me."

Kat looked at Simon, who took his place beside Gabrielle. "I'm not going back to those mosquitoes."

She turned to Hale, who didn't say a thing. He just pulled her phone from her pocket and handed it to Gabrielle. "Make the call."

Kat watched her cousin dial, heard her say, "Hey, Mom. Yeah, I don't think I can make it to Paraguay. See, I met this duke..."

A few moments later, the phone was passed to Simon, who left a message for his father about a lecture he just had to hear at MIT.

Kat knew the argument was over. The job, however, was only just beginning, so she turned to Hale and asked, "Where's the hotel?"

"Well, see, I thought *hotel* was really more of a suggestion and..." He turned and pointed to a long pier, a bobbing motorboat, and Marcus, who stood to attention, waiting.

"What's that?" Kat asked.

"That's our ride."

5 DAYS UNTIL
THE AUCTION

ABOARD THE *W. W. HALE,*
SOMEWHERE OFF THE
COAST OF MONACO

TWENTY

Katarina Bishop did not always land on her feet. She'd had a lot of identities, it was true, but she didn't have nine lives. So it was with great amusement the next morning that Simon and Hale sat on the beautifully appointed deck furniture, staring at the clear blue water of the Mediterranean, and Simon said, "What do you mean, Kat's afraid of water?"

"Terrified." Hale sounded like someone who desperately wanted to be serious. But couldn't.

Kat tried to protest, but that would have required stepping out onto the deck. And the deck had the rail. And if the rail failed, the deck also had a long drop to water and a longer swim to shore; so Kat was quite happy listening from inside, thank you very much.

Simon turned and yelled through the open sliding doors to where Kat stood, regretting that she'd ever got onto that boat or out of bed.

"Are you really that afraid of water?"

"I'm not afraid of water, Simon," Kat yelled back. "I'm afraid of drowning. There's a difference."

"I thought you knew how to swim," Gabrielle said, stretching out on one of the chaise longues, handing Simon a bottle of suntan lotion, and rolling onto her stomach in the universal signal for *Do my back*.

"Of course I can swim. I can also remember a very unfortunate incident involving Uncle Louie, the Bagshaws and a cruise ship off the coast of Belize."

"You're fine, Kitty Kat." Gabrielle slipped on a pair of dark sunglasses and the largest, floppiest hat that Kat had ever seen, and it occurred to her for one brief second how spoiled she really was. After all, there are worse things than spending the end of February on a private yacht in the middle of the Mediterranean with friends and family (especially, let's face it, with friends who look like Hale).

She stole a glance at him. *I kissed Hale.* Then the boat listed gently, and Kat's empty stomach swayed. She honestly thought she might be sick.

"If anything happens, Marcus will save you. Won't you, Marcus?" Hale asked, looking up at the man, who nodded.

"It would be an honour, miss."

"Let's try not to let it come to that," Kat said, bravely making her way across the deck and gently lowering herself into one of the chairs at the table. She gripped the arms of the chair a little too tightly as Marcus poured her a cup of tea and placed a chocolate croissant on the plate before her.

The motion was so smooth, so effortless, that Kat had to think – not for the first time – that Marcus would have made a most excellent thief. But Marcus was the one person Kat knew who had the skills but not the heart. It was only one of many reasons she liked him.

"I trust the lady slept well?" Marcus asked.

"Yeah," Hale asked, grinning. "How did the lady sleep?"

"I asked for a hotel, Hale. Not a penthouse. Not even a suite. Just one little hotel room on dry land."

"Call me crazy, Kat." Hale held his arms out wide. "But I thought *this* was better."

Beyond him, Kat saw the white yachts that bobbed up and down in Hercules Harbour, and the tall stone cliffs that formed the rocky barricade between Monaco and France. To her right, she could see all the way to Italy. To her left was Saint-Tropez. The *W. W. Hale* was two hundred and twenty feet of highly polished luxury, and Kat sat surrounded by blue waters and clear sky and the infinite possibility that comes with almost limitless wealth.

But Kat had far more pressing matters on her mind when she turned to Simon. "What do we know?"

"I think you should apologise to my ship first," Hale said before Simon could answer.

"Hale..."

"She's a very nice yacht, you know. I won her from a Colombian coffee baron in a game of high-stakes poker."

"Your grandfather gave it to your father for his birthday."

Hale shrugged. "Same difference. You still need to apologise."

"Hale!" Kat cried, but the boy only stared at her. "Fine," she conceded. "I love your boat."

"Ship."

"Ship... Your ship is beautiful."

He smiled as if to say he approved, then reached for the pastries, broke off a corner of a pain au chocolat, and plopped it into his mouth.

"So what do we know?" Kat asked again.

"What do you think?" Hale smirked and picked up a nearby newspaper. The pages crackled as he turned them.

"I think first they're going to have to get it authenticated," Kat said.

"Give the lady a prize." Hale took a long sip of orange juice. "Right, Simon?"

The smaller boy nodded and settled as far under an umbrella as he could get. "The best I can tell, they've got a bunch of experts flying in – a lot of the same people Kelly just used in New York. Two antiquities experts from the Egyptian Museum in Cairo. The gemologist from India, and a handful of others."

"Is that a party we can crash?" Kat asked.

Simon shrugged. "Maybe. They're being really...careful."

"I'm sure they are," Kat and Gabrielle said at the same time.

"There's just one problem." Hale stood and strolled to the serving area and poured himself a cup of steaming coffee. "These experts that Simon's talking about, don't you think that one of them will notice that this long-lost, world-famous emerald is exactly like the other world-famous emerald they just examined?"

Gabrielle lowered her sunglasses and studied Kat, the two cousins sharing an *Oh, isn't he adorable* look.

Hale dropped back into his chair, blew on his coffee, and said, "What?"

"The Cleopatra is locked away on the other side of the ocean, behind heat-sensitive security cameras and several inches of bulletproof glass," Simon reminded them, but Hale just looked at Kat.

"Ninety per cent of the con is the story," she told him. "And the Antony Emerald..." She couldn't help herself, she sighed. "That's a story they *want* to believe."

Kat looked down at the newspapers and magazines that covered the table, all with the same pictures – the same story – that the Antony Emerald had been found.

"She's really good," Kat whispered almost to herself.

"So are we," Hale said.

Kat felt the blood go to her cheeks and told herself it was the heat, the sun. But when Hale leaned close to her, staring, searching her eyes, Kat knew it was really the kiss.

She looked down at the pictures of Maggie and the emerald. And then her gaze locked upon the shorter-than-average man in a nicer-than-average suit who appeared in the background of almost every single frame.

"Him. The guy from the press conference..." Kat pointed to the man with the bifocals and the accent. "From what I can tell, he hasn't left her side since she got here. So exactly what does Monsieur LaFont know about our emerald?"

Gabrielle sat upright. Simon looked up from the laptop's

screen. Hale raised one eyebrow and whispered, "There's one way to find out."

TWENTY-ONE

Pierre LaFont was not unknown to the men and women who worked at L'Hôtel Royal de Monaco. He had single-handedly selected the chandelier that hung in the recently renovated Royal Suite. He frequently dined in the hotel's restaurant with visiting dignitaries and the occasional heiress who was in the market to either buy or sell. But as the valet held his car door open that Sunday morning, there was something different about the Monsieur LaFont who stepped into the bright sun, a copy of the morning paper tucked beneath his arm, photo out.

"*Bonjour,*" he said, tipping his hat to a wealthy woman waiting for the valet. "*Bonjour,*" he told the bellman who stood beside the revolving doors.

"Now, that is a beautiful automobile."

It was a by-product of the business that LaFont's first instinct was to size and frame. As he turned at the voice, he expected to see the custom-made suit and expensive watch. The young man who had spoken had the wide smile and confident ease that often comes with wealth and privilege.

But studying him in the morning light, there was something about the young man, LaFont thought, that was quite uncommon indeed.

"Is it a '58?" the young man asked. His hands were deep in his pockets as he stepped out of the shadows and onto the cobblestone street, examining the old Porsche Speedster with a discerning eye.

"It is," Pierre said.

"Nothing takes a curve quite like it," the young man said.

"You know the '58 Speedster?" Pierre asked in the manner of a man who appreciates people who appreciate things.

"I do." The young man placed one arm around LaFont's shoulders, and with the other, patted the man twice on the chest. "But I'd keep this one away from fountains if I were you. Water does terrible things to the upholstery."

"Pardon?" Pierre asked, but the young man just waved the words away and reached for the hotel door.

"Never mind, Mr LaFont. Never mind."

The Long Con is a misnomer, Kat had always thought. Nothing in her world was ever truly long term, least of all the jobs themselves. Even the longest con was never more than an assortment of moments that were, in themselves, very, very short; or so she had to think as she stood watching Hale and Pierre LaFont in the foyer of the grand hotel below.

It had taken Hale no more than a second to pick the older man's pocket. It was the blink of an eye before Hale passed LaFont's phone to Gabrielle. Less than a minute later, Simon had swapped out the phone's SIM card and done something very tricky with a laptop and a long wire and then given the device back to Gabrielle.

So, no, Kat was convinced, cons were never long. They were measured in the beats of a heart, and if in those moments, the mark looked the wrong way or the guard glanced up at the wrong time, then everything could go terribly, terribly wrong.

Kat knew these things, of course, but never had they been quite as evident as when she looked back to the revolving door and saw two tall, lanky and very familiar figures appear.

"Oh, no," she muttered to no one but herself, but it was already too late.

Hale was with Pierre LaFont, trying to rope him in. Gabrielle was halfway across the lobby, LaFont's phone in her outstretched hand. So Kat was the one who bolted from the railing and ran down the stairs, knowing in her heart that it was too late long before she heard the loud voice call out, "Gabs!"

The Scottish accent was thicker than Kat remembered, but it was a voice that she didn't think she'd ever forget (even though she wasn't exactly sure which of the ruddy-faced figures had yelled).

They were walking away from her and moving quickly. It seemed to Kat as if they'd each grown a foot in the two months since she'd last seen them settled on opposite sides of Uncle Eddie's kitchen table. Angus was still taller, but not by much. Hamish's shoulders were even wider than his brother's. And it was a laugh of pure joy that came from both of them as they saw Gabrielle walking silently and purposefully across the floor. She was shifting LaFont's phone to her left hand. She was eyeing the inner pocket of the man's well-cut suit. Gabrielle's thoughts and gaze and step were locked on one purpose, and Kat knew there was no way she would see the danger that was ten feet away and closing in fast.

"Gabrielle!" Kat said, rushing across the floor. But any hope that tragedy might be avoided went away with the booming voice that drowned out her own, crying, "Gabby!"

No one would ever know how much blame should be placed on the curse, and what, if any, should lie firmly on the shoulders of the Bagshaws. All Kat knew for certain was that Angus had broken into a run and was throwing his arms around Gabrielle, lifting her off her feet and squeezing her tightly.

Through the comms unit in her ear, Kat heard LaFont saying, "Thank you very much, young man, but I'm afraid I have a pressing appointment with Maggie now."

She watched Hale's eyes go wide as he finally saw the way Gabrielle's long legs dangled inches from the floor as first Angus and then Hamish took turns spinning her around.

Kat listened to the crash as the cell phone fell from Gabrielle's hand and onto the polished floor, sliding, skidding across the marble.

She held her breath as it zoomed underneath a bellman's rolling cart, barely missing the wheels. Kat could have sworn her heart stopped beating as a businessman stepped over it, completely unaware that it was there. It seemed to take forever for the phone to come to rest beneath the cloth that covered a long table not ten feet from where LaFont and Hale stood.

"Why, is that Hale I see over—" Hamish started to yell in Hale's direction, but Gabrielle's foot jabbed into his shin, cutting him off mid-sentence.

A hotel employee stood right beside the table where the phone had disappeared, and Kat ran to him. "Oh my gosh!" she exclaimed. "Are those two boys attacking that pretty girl?" she cried, pointing to where Hamish was rubbing his shin and Angus was still hugging Gabrielle, sweeping her long legs back and forth across the floor.

"You there!" the employee cried without a second glance at the young woman who had already dropped to her knees and reached under the cloth.

"Where is it?" Kat said to no one but herself. The floor was hard on her knees. It was cool against her hands. And still Kat crawled, looking, searching. Praying.

"Where is it?" she said again as she crawled, shrouded in the shadows, closer to the phone, but also to LaFont and Hale...

And the big brassy voice that yelled, "LaFont, you rascal!"

Kat picked up the hem of the cloth and peered outside just in time to see Hale disappear out of the front door and Pierre turn and say, "*Bonjour*, Madame Maggie."

Kat didn't let herself panic. The dread she was feeling was too great, the worry too strong, and it was entirely too useless a thing to do. She did allow herself to think *What else can go wrong?* which, of course, was exactly when the elevator doors opened and an attendant ushered LaFont and Maggie inside...

And the phone began to ring.

Kat lunged for it, tried to muffle the sound, but the harm was done, and LaFont was already stopping, patting his pockets. Searching.

"You wouldn't keep a lady waiting, would you, Pierre?" Maggie asked in her thick Texas drawl.

"My apologies, Madame. I just can't seem to find my phone."

With the words, a faint crack appeared in Maggie's smooth façade. "Your phone is missing?"

"Well...not missing. I hear the thing, you see."

In the next moment, Kat was out from under the table and the phone was in her hand. She could see them moving into the elevators. She felt the seconds passing.

The seconds.

Always a matter of seconds.

And that was how long it took for Kat to call out, "Hello, Maggie."

TWENTY-TWO

Kat should have been terrified, but she wasn't. She should have turned and run, but she didn't. All she could really do was look down at the phone that had suddenly stopped ringing and keep her steady pace across the lobby floor.

"Oh, Maggie," she cried one more time for good measure. "Wait for me!"

Even the voices in her ear were quiet, her crew silent as she walked to the elevator and stepped inside as if she rode to penthouses on the Riviera every day (which hadn't been true, strictly speaking, since the summer she'd turned thirteen).

Sometimes a con has to run. Sometimes a thief needs to hide. But as she gripped LaFont's now-silent cell phone in her left fist and took her place in the elevator at Maggie's side, Kat took a deep breath and told herself that a thief's greatest skill is the ability to adapt.

She turned to the woman beside her and said, "Hello, Maggie."

Kat felt LaFont watching her, so she turned. "Hi. I'm Kat."

"Kat is—" Maggie started.

"A member of the family," Kat finished.

Maggie smiled. "Indeed."

"Pierre LaFont," LaFont said. Kat placed her hand gently in his palm, and he kissed the top of it. "A pleasure, my dear."

"Did you hear that, Aunt Maggie? I'm a pleasure," Kat said.

"Yes, dear," Maggie said as the elevator reached the penthouse. "I've known that for some—"

But then the elevator jerked to a stop. Maggie faltered. Kat stumbled. And Pierre LaFont never felt the small hand that slipped his cell phone back into the side pocket of his impeccably tailored suit coat.

The man smiled down at Kat, oblivious, and gestured towards the open doors. "After you."

Kat was not unfamiliar with hotel suites. She'd spent too much of her youth with her father. She'd spent too much time lately with Hale. So she should have felt at home among the lovely linens and priceless views, but that time, of course, she didn't.

"Pierre, you're gonna have to give us a minute, darling." Maggie put her arm around Kat's shoulders and gripped her tightly. "I'm gonna have to go figure out a way to put some meat on these little bones."

She squeezed tighter. Kat grinned wider. And then Maggie was pushing Kat into a small study and pulling shut the sliding doors. An old-fashioned key was in the lock, and Maggie turned it. In the silence of the rich panelled room, it made an ominous sound.

"Well, if it isn't Katarina Bishop..."

The change was so quick, so effortless, it was like flipping a switch. The brass Texas twang was gone, replaced by an accent that *was* English, but it wasn't the voice that Kat had heard in the diner, either. Kat was standing across from the woman for the fourth time, but now Maggie appeared younger than she'd looked in New York; she seemed more regal than she'd been in the hotel lobby. Leaning against the big double doors, there wasn't a doubt in Kat's mind that she was finally face-to-face with the woman behind the con.

"Hello, Maggie," Kat said. "Or should I call you Constance?"

The woman smiled. "Call me Maggie."

Maggie walked to the sideboard and poured a drink. She offered the glass to Kat, then pulled it back. "Oops," she said with a condescending smile. "I forgot. You're a child."

"Is that why you did it?"

"Don't you mean, is that why you were such an easy mark?"

Kat wished there was something she could say to prove that the woman was wrong, but there was no use.

"Age does not make the mark, Katarina. Surely dear Edward has taught you that?"

At the mention of Uncle Eddie, Kat felt her pulse race, her stomach turn; and Maggie must have seen it, because she smiled. "So tell me, where is Edward these days?"

"Paraguay." Kat had to think. "Or Uruguay..."

Maggie chuckled and took a drink. "I get them confused."

"Me too," Kat confided. She looked around. "Speaking of

family, where's your '*grandson*'?"

"Who?" Maggie asked, then she seemed to remember the woman she'd been a few days before. "Oh, him... He was the help, dear. Someone who is useful on occasion, but not really at *our* level." She held her glass towards Kat – a toast. "You are a very gifted girl, Katarina. Has anyone told you that?"

Kat was sure her father or Uncle Eddie must have said the words at some point, but she couldn't remember where or when.

Maggie eyed her. "How old were you when you went on your first job?"

"Three," Kat said.

"I was nine." Maggie leaned against the rounded arm of a leather chair. "It was the jewellery counter at Harrods department store on the day before Christmas." She touched the diamond studs in her ears. "I still wear them, see?"

"They're beautiful," Kat said.

The woman smiled. "Thank you." She sank slowly into the chair. "There are too few of us girls in the Old Boys' Club, I think." She took a slow drink, then fingered the rim of her crystal glass. "Even fewer Old Girls."

Kat had never known her grandmother. Her mother had been taken from her far too soon, and yet it had never occurred to her until then that there might be something – someone – missing from Uncle Eddie's kitchen table. But watching Maggie touch the stones in her ears, Kat knew the con was over. There was no angle, no job, no lie – only a woman who could have been there. But wasn't. The absence was like a gaping hole inside Kat's chest.

"How do you know him?" Kat had to know. "Why haven't I ever met you before? Why aren't you—"

"Part of the family?" Maggie guessed. Kat nodded, too tongue-tied to speak. "That is a long story, my dear, and one that I will not be telling," Maggie said simply. "Besides, I do my best work alone. I'm sure you understand."

"I see."

"I heard about Moscow, by the way. It was—"

"Risky, I know," Kat said, unable to bear another lecture.

But Maggie just shook her head. Her eyes sparkled. "It was exactly what I would have done."

When Maggie raised her eyebrows, she appeared younger than Kat had seen her yet. Age is just a number, after all. Youth is something else, and Kat could see that there – in the middle of the con – Maggie was turning back the clock, and Kat envied her. She thought of Gabrielle's words and wondered if she was really looking at the female Uncle Eddie. Or maybe Kat was simply seeing the thief Kat herself might grow up to someday be.

"Personally, I love a Cézanne," Maggie said longingly, and raised her glass again. "So I, of course, wouldn't have given it away."

And just like that the spell was broken. The last few days came rushing back, and there was only one thing about the woman that mattered. When Kat spoke again, she couldn't hide her disappointment. "You broke the rules, Maggie."

"There is no honour among thieves, Katarina. No matter

what you might have read in storybooks." She smiled a terribly wicked smile. "Part of the fun is getting the best of our rivals."

"You said Romani sent you."

Maggie waved the concern away. "I played the mark."

"You used a Chelovek Pseudonima for your own purposes."

Maggie pointed a finger at Kat, as if she'd just realised something. "I was once young like you – so fiery, so passionate. When I heard about the Henley…I was impressed. That was very nice work, Katarina." If she expected Kat to acknowledge the compliment, she was mistaken. "And then I started hearing stories of other jobs…and I knew that you had become noble. It is an adorable look on you. It goes with your eyes. You can tell your uncle that."

"Uncle Eddie isn't part of this."

Maggie laughed. "Well, if Eddie didn't send you, then who did?"

"Visily Romani."

Maggie laughed harder. "Well, I'm here on behalf of the Easter Bunny, so—"

"We're going to get it back, you know?"

Maggie nodded slowly. There was a harsh, sudden edge to her voice when she said, "You're going to try."

Rich, dense curtains blocked out the sun. It was quiet – almost peaceful – in the dim room, and Kat thought she heard her own heart pounding as she sat listening to Maggie say, "I'm very proud of you for coming here, Katarina. I would have found it insulting if you'd insisted on skulking around in the shadows as if I wouldn't see you - as if I wouldn't hear you."

"Well, as long as you're not offended..."

"So what would you like, dear? Ten per cent?"

Kat didn't even do the mental maths - she didn't dare. "That's so nice of you to offer, but I think I'll just take it all."

Maggie threw her head back and laughed. "So you're going to try...what? Birds of a Feather?" she guessed.

"Of course not," Kat said. "Everyone knows the French government banned the importation of peacocks in 1987."

"True." Maggie frowned as if that particular development had caused her a great deal of grief on many occasions. "London Bridge?" she guessed, but Kat said nothing. "A Jack and Jill?"

"Well, it is one of Hale's favourites," Kat managed to quip. "He makes an excellent Jill."

"I don't doubt it."

Kat felt a little dizzy, watching her options fall away like the shattered panes of a broken window. She feared she might get cut.

"So what *is* your play, Katarina?" Maggie poured herself another drink and sipped, her lips pursed against the crystal rim. "What is the master plan of the master thief who robbed the Henley?"

Kat prayed that her silence would read as strength instead of weakness, wisdom instead of foolishness. Most of all, she wished she knew the answer to that very question. But she didn't. So instead she just said, "You shouldn't have gone after the Cleopatra. You shouldn't have used me to do it. But your biggest mistake was using the name Romani. When this is over, you'll know that was where you blew it."

"You're good, Katarina. You really are. A bit reckless, though. And entirely too gullible. It's a shame there is so much your family has failed to teach you. There's so much I could teach you."

"The thing you're forgetting, Mags, is even if we can't steal the Cleopatra back, that doesn't mean you can sell it – not before I call New York and suggest that the Kelly Corporation run a few tests on the stone they've got under glass."

"You won't do that, Katarina."

"Oh, believe me, Maggie. I would."

Kat didn't smile because she was gloating. It was simply the smile of someone who has made her peace with her mistakes and is prepared to live with consequences. But then Maggie joined her, a phone in her hand.

"I do love the new technologies," she said, smiling down at the device. "They've made certain elements of our profession much more challenging, don't get me wrong, but some things..." Her voice trailed off as she pressed a button. The tiny screen was instantly filled with a small but perfectly clear picture: Marcus and Hale outside the Kelly Corporation. Then the image changed, and Kat saw Hale and Gabrielle walking into the corporate headquarters in full dress and mid-con.

There were at least a half dozen images, but it was the final one that caused Kat's heart to stop.

A small park. A quiet day. Maggie brought one heavily jewelled finger to the screen and said, "That's me. That's you." Finally the fingernail came to rest on the envelope in the centre of the screen, passing between the two of them. "And that is you giving me the Cleopatra Emerald."

Maggie walked to the door and turned the key, then glanced back to the girl by the window.

"Do think about what I said, Katarina. I'd be most happy to teach you all I know."

TWENTY-THREE

The tide was low off the coast of Monaco that Friday evening when the *W. W. Hale* pulled away from the long row of yachts that were an almost permanent part of the shore. The moon was only a tiny sliver as it rose in the distance over Italy. Everything, it seemed, was at its lowest as Kat stood in the doorway of the ship's galley kitchen and said, "It's over."

The big door on the Sub-Zero refrigerator slammed closed, and Hale turned to Kat, a look on his face that was somewhere between rage and relief. Gabrielle had a new scrape on the side of her face and ice on her knee. The Bagshaws stood together beside Simon, who was still slowly sorting through Interpol's files – face by face, job by job.

Kat smiled despite herself at the sight of them. "So...the gang's all here."

"Hey, Kitty," Angus said.

"Sorry for getting in the way, Kat." Hamish eased closer. He seemed even taller and significantly wider. She wondered for a second what he'd been eating to grow so big. "If we'd known you guys were pulling a job, we never would have blown into town unannounced and—"

"It's OK, guys. Really." Kat climbed onto one of the stools that lined the granite-covered bar. It felt harder than it should have to pull herself up. "It's over. It's fine. I'm assuming they filled you in?"

The Bagshaws had never been ones for overthinking, and Kat highly doubted they were going to start then.

"Sure did, Kitty!" Hamish threw his arm around her. Angus joined from the other side, squeezing until she hurt.

"We heard you were in Edinburgh in January," Angus said. "But you didn't call."

"You didn't write," his brother added.

"Don't feel bad, boys," Hale said from across the galley. "She doesn't call anyone any more."

Part of being a great thief means seeing what isn't there – the hidden sensor or invisible grid, the lie a guard really, really wants to believe. So Kat knew what Hale was saying; she'd heard it on an escalator and in the backseat of a chauffeured car, on the brownstone stairs, and now, half a world away.

"Don't be angry, Hale."

"You went off script today," he snapped.

"We were blown."

"And you got in a lift with that woman. Alone."

"I'm a big girl, Hale," Kat said. "Besides, she's not going to hurt me."

"We don't know that," Hale shot back. "We don't know anything about her."

"Yes." Kat had to laugh. "We do. I've known her my whole

life. Sure –" she added before he could cut her off – "I *met* her two weeks ago, but I know her." Kat thought about Maggie at the age of nine, pulling a diamond heist at Harrods. "I know her very, very well."

Angus looked at Hamish. "I hate it when Mum and Dad fight."

Hamish smoothed his brother's messy hair. "Me too."

It was then that Marcus appeared in the room. His dark suit coat was gone, and he wore the sleeves of his white shirt rolled up to just below his elbows. Kat might have joked about the display of skin were it not for the neat apron he wore and the sense of purpose he exuded as he walked to the wide stove top and took the cover from a large Dutch oven. Steam billowed from the pot, and Kat closed her eyes. Instead of the smooth cool granite, her fingers felt rough old wood. They were at sea on the other side of the world, but with one deep breath, Kat was sitting at her uncle's table.

The child who had never had a house felt homesick. The thief who had robbed the Henley wanted help. And the girl who'd walked away from her family business came to realise that, no matter what she did, she never could leave the kitchen.

"So...someone stole the Cleopatra," Hamish said, as if he couldn't take the silence one minute more.

His brother gave a low whistle and shook his head. "Wish we'd been around for that."

"No." Gabrielle repositioned her ice pack. "You don't."

"Angus," Kat said, turning to the brothers. "Hamish,

her real accent is English. Do you know her?"

The two brothers stared, each daring the other to speak.

"No," Hamish said softly.

"How bad is it?" Hale asked her.

"Bad," Kat said. She stared down at the granite, trying to find a pattern in the specks of light and dark, but there was no sense to be found in it. "We're blown. She knows both of you." She pointed between Hale and Gabrielle.

"She doesn't know me," Simon said.

Kat laughed. "I think we should assume she knows everyone. It would be like..." She shook her head, tried to bring her mind back into focus.

"Uncle Eddie," Gabrielle finally finished for her. "It would be like trying to con Uncle Eddie."

"Yeah," Kat said. "She knows...everything."

"Like what?" Gabrielle asked.

"Like who we are... Like why we're here... Like every con we could possibly run to get the emerald back..."

"So?" Hale asked.

"So she's better than I am!"

Part of Kat hoped that at least one member of her crew would exclaim, *Of course not!* Another part of her presumed that someone might say, *Don't be ridiculous.* But no one quoted her résumé. Not a soul mentioned the Henley.

"We can't do it," Kat admitted slowly. "We just can't... win."

Hamish smiled and rubbed his hands together. "Sure we can. What do you say? Pigs in a Blanket?" He leaned over the cool counter and raised his eyebrows at Gabrielle.

"The only way I'll get under a blanket with you is if both of us are on fire," she told him.

"You guys don't get it," Kat snapped. "We can't con her. She *knows* all the old cons. She probably invented half of them."

"So we think of some new ones." Gabrielle rose.

"She knows *us*." Kat looked at Hale.

"So we don't rely on us," Hale countered.

"She knows Uncle Eddie. I'd bet money she knows everyone we know."

Hale moved closer. "So we find someone she doesn't know."

The ship was moving, slipping further and further from the shore, and yet it felt as if the whole world was watching. The kitchen was too crowded. Kat's stomach turned, and so she kept her gaze on Hale, as if he were a solid point on the horizon that she was going to focus on until she could no longer feel the yacht rock or sway.

"We're going to find someone she doesn't know," Hale said again.

Right then, Kat swore she wouldn't look away for anything, but that was before she heard the footsteps, saw the shadow in the doorway, and heard the voice that asked, "You mean someone like me?"

TWENTY-FOUR

The first time Kat had seen the boy who stood framed in the doorway, they'd both been standing on a street corner in Paris. Their first conversation had been over a picked lock and a picked pocket, and Kat had had a sneaking suspicion that she was in the room with someone with a great deal of natural talent and the subsequent disrespect for laws and truth. But those weren't the moments that came to Kat's mind as the whole room stood staring, waiting to see what other surprises might be lurking on the other side of that door.

"What?" Nick asked, looking at the awestruck teens. "You can't recognise me when you aren't leaving me in a locked gallery for the police to find?"

"Oh, don't be silly, Nicholas," Gabrielle said, casually inspecting her nails. "We knew museum security would find you long before the cops did."

"Sweet as always, Gabrielle." Nick nodded at the girl, then turned to Simon and the Bagshaws. "Fellas...sorry to barge in."

"I think the technical term is *stow away*," Hale said.

Nick snapped his fingers. "I think you're right."

"What?" Hale looked him up and down. "No wet suit?"

"Didn't want to mess up my hair," Nick said with a smile.

And through it all, Kat sat speechless.

"Boys, boys," Gabrielle said, leaning against the counter like a jazz singer from the thirties. "Play nice."

"I am nice," Hale said, but his voice was made of glass. "I was just about to ask our old friend Nick how Paris is these days."

"Lyon," Nick corrected. "My mom's at Interpol head-quarters now." His gaze slid sideways to Kat. "Or didn't you know?"

He sounded perfectly straight when he said it, and that was when Kat realised two very important things: the first was that Nick was going to keep her secret. The second was that Nick...was good. She wasn't sure which she wanted to think about, so instead she just said, "How long have you been here?"

"Long enough."

"And exactly *why* are you here?" Kat asked. "The last time you offered your services, I seem to remember you secretly planning to catch us all red-handed and turn us over to Interpol. Or are you out of your family business?"

Kat saw her reflection in the windows. There was nothing beyond the glass but an empty expanse of black.

"Maybe I switched sides." Nick ran a hand along the granite island. "Maybe I came all this way to help you steal the Antony Emerald."

"It's not the Antony," Hale corrected.

"Interpol sent a team to help authenticate it," Nick told them. "It's real, Kat."

"Oh, it's a real emerald, all right," Gabrielle said, then smiled smugly. "It's just not the Antony."

"No," Nick said. "Can't be. The only other emerald that size is..."

"Oh yeah. It's the Cleopatra," Gabrielle told him.

"How do you know?" Nick asked.

"We know," Kat said slowly, "because we're the ones who stole it."

Lying awake in the king-size bed she shared with Gabrielle, Kat stared up at the chandelier that hung overhead, watched it sway like a pendulum with the waves.

When she tossed and turned, she tried to blame the sea. When sleep didn't come, she wanted to think it was because of Gabrielle's snoring. But when Gabrielle began to kick, Kat knew there was no use in fighting. A fully conscious Gabrielle was a force to be reckoned with. A sleeping (and possibly cursed) Gabrielle was a whole other level of dangerous, so Kat slipped from the bed and quietly towards the door.

The phone was right where she'd left it. The number was one she knew by heart. And as she stepped out onto the deck, she realised it was early evening in Paraguay. Or was it Uruguay? It didn't really matter, Kat thought as she stood, waiting to be able to say, "Hi, Daddy."

"What's wrong?" he asked, and Kat laughed.

"Nothing. I just—"

"Kat, what is wrong?"

"I missed you. Is missing you not allowed?"

"No, it is allowed. In fact, it's my preference. But you don't exactly have a track record of preferential behaviour."

Kat leaned against the railing and whispered, "I miss you."

"You said that already," her father told her from the other side of the world.

"Yeah, but this time I really mean it."

"So, word on the street is that your cousin has conned you into something with a count."

"A duke," Kat corrected. "We're—"

"So what are you *really* doing?"

"Scoping the caves around Zurich, looking for a Degas no one's seen in sixty years."

She could almost imagine the smile on her father's face when he said, "That's my girl."

It was too cold on the deck, and Kat wished she'd brought a jacket, wished she'd waited for the sun. She imagined her father, tanned and tired and happy. She thought of Maggie, and for a second, considered begging for forgiveness or pleading for help, but Kat couldn't do either. She had too much of her uncle's pride, too little of her father's charm. Kat was just...Kat – chasing after the past, and doing it, for better or worse, all on her own.

* * *

After she had said goodbye to her father, Kat stayed outside for a long time, staring at the water.

"Don't fall in."

Kat jumped at the sound of Hale's voice, then slowly turned to face him.

"Don't say that. With the way our luck is going, at least one of us is bound to end up overboard before this thing is through."

She felt him come to stand beside her, taking his place at the rail.

"So what are you doing out here in the middle of the night?"

"Thinking."

"See." Hale pointed at her. "Right there. That is your problem."

It was long past midnight, and the Mediterranean waters looked like ink as they lapped against the *W. W. Hale*'s white hull. The lights of places like Saint-Tropez and Nice were tiny diamonds in the distance, and it felt to Kat as if she and Hale were closer to the moon than any other living soul or thing.

"You didn't hear her today, Hale. She's so...good."

"You said that."

"She's seen everything. She's done everything. Hey –" she pointed at him – "maybe a Catherine the Great? You know, Uncle Felix posed as a curator at the Cairo Museum one year, and—"

"For a while there, it looked like you were giving up on this," he whispered.

"I know, but I thought that if we—"

"Kat..."

"Yes?"

"Stop thinking."

Of all the things that had been asked of Kat in her fifteen years, that was perhaps the hardest. But she tried – she really did. To forget about the lapping waves and deep blue water. To ignore the ticking clock, the mounting odds, and the tiny voice in the back of her mind saying, *I kissed you. I kissed you. I kissed you.*

And you left.

"You're the only friend I've ever had, Hale. You know that, right?"

"Don't lie—"

Kat shook her head. "If I were lying, it would sound a lot better than that." She saw Hale draw a breath and ease towards her, but Kat talked on. "In my family, we take our cons seriously, you know? Like Grandmother's pearls, or the good china. They've been handed down for years. Centuries. Someone taught Uncle Eddie, and Uncle Eddie taught my mom. And Mom taught Dad, and Dad taught—"

"You."

"Yeah," Kat admitted while Hale inched closer.

"And you taught me."

Kat laughed and turned back to the water. "Sorry about that."

But Hale wasn't laughing when he said, "I'm not."

Standing there in the moonlight, Kat saw him set his jaw

and turn towards her.

"Someone did them first, Kat. Don't forget that. Someone, somewhere did them first." He shrugged. "So we'll do something first. Who knows? Maybe a hundred years from now, two crazy kids will be debating the merits of the Kat in the Hat."

"Really? That's the name you're going with?"

He laughed and gripped the rail. "It's a work in progress."

Out on the water, without the heat of the sun, Kat's breath fogged in the chilly air.

"Do you think it's real?" he asked.

"I know it's real. I'm the one who carried it out of the heating duct, remember?"

She shivered, and Hale placed his arms around her, gripping the rail on either side, pressing her tight between the cool rail and the warmth of his chest. "Not the Cleopatra – the Antony. Do you think it's out there somewhere?"

"Do you think that two thousand years ago there was an emerald so big you could cut it in half and get two stones that size?"

"Do you think there was a love so big it could curse anyone who went against it?"

"It's just a story, Hale."

"Yeah, but it's a *good* story. Isn't it?"

He squeezed her as if forcing out an answer.

"I don't know. I mean, it's kind of silly."

"Silly? Not the word I usually associate with the power couple of the Roman Empire, but whatever."

"I mean, she was Cleopatra... Shouldn't she and Antony have known better? They were so different..."

"Variety is the spice of life."

"And from a thousand miles apart."

"Absence makes the heart grow fonder."

"And doomed."

She strongly suspected his mind was on anything but Cleopatra when he let her go and asked, "Don't you mean scared?"

Kat felt her heart beat faster, adrenaline pumping through her veins, and she knew he was right. She studied him for a long time. "Do you believe in curses, Hale?"

He looked at her. "I believe in you."

4 DAYS BEFORE
THE AUCTION

THE *W. W. HALE,*
SOMEWHERE OFF THE
COAST OF MONACO

TWENTY-FIVE

Perhaps it was the crisp wind and the clear sun that greeted them on the deck early the next morning (though Kat chose to credit Marcus's excellent coffee), but the fact remained that by seven a.m., Kat and her crew were especially...awake.

Nick sat beside Simon, who was at his computer. Marcus stood at attention beside the food. Hale had his feet on the table, reading the morning paper.

And someone had given the Bagshaws a gun.

"Pull!" Hamish yelled, and Angus pulled a cord and sent a skeet flying across the deep blue water.

A split second later, a loud crack was reverberating across the deck. Kat jumped. Hale sighed. The shot went far wide, and Marcus never moved a muscle.

Kat took the seat on the other side of Simon. "Good morning," she told him and risked a glance at the screen, but Simon said nothing. "Simon..." she tried again, but Hale cut her off with a slight shake of his head.

"Thinking," he whispered.

Kat waited.

She didn't sip the coffee. She didn't take a bite of the fluffy roll. She just sat watching Simon's eyes.

"Yes!" he yelled and pumped his fist in the air while, behind him, Angus took the gun and yelled, "Pull!"

"So, Simon..." Kat leaned over the table, and Simon finally seemed to realise he wasn't alone.

"Hey, Kat."

Kat chuckled. "Hey. So what's new?" She eyed the computer and the smile that spread across Simon's face.

"Well...see...you know the bug we put in LaFont's phone yesterday?"

"The one that made Kat blow our cover?" Gabrielle asked, strolling onto the deck and over to one of the chaise longues.

"Yes, that one," Kat conceded.

"PULL!"

Crack.

Again, the shot went wide, and again, the brothers hardly noticed.

"What about it, Simon?" Hale asked, his eyes hidden behind dark glasses, and yet Kat was certain that his gaze never trailed from where Nick sat on the other side of the table.

"Yeah, well, the new phones are really more like little computers and..."

"Simon. Buddy," Hale prompted.

"We didn't just bug his phone. This morning, LaFont synced his phone to his computer."

"So we..." Kat prompted.

"We have everything." Simon turned the screen around.

"'Today, three o'clock, photo op at the Prince's Palace,'" he read. "'Four forty-five, interview with Maggie and the Associated Press. Seven p.m., polishing with the royal jeweller... Tomorrow, nine a.m., VIP brunch with, what...three CEOs, the Russian ambassador, a delegation from Egypt. Ooh, Princess Ann of Astovia – I hear her plastic surgery was very effective."

Nick gave a low whistle then settled back in his chair. "This is a very busy emerald."

"Looks like it all culminates Thursday night with a big ball or gala or whatever," Simon said, and Gabrielle looked offended that galas and balls could ever be *whatever*ed away. "The emerald is going to be there so all the potential bidders can see it up close. Then Friday morning, they auction it off."

"You've got locations?" Kat asked Simon.

"Oh, yeah. We've got everything."

"Security?"

"If LaFont knows it, we know it."

It felt as if maybe the curse had lifted, the tide had shifted, but then the breeze picked up and a skeet took a very unfortunate turn. Seconds later, Angus was pulling his shot far to the right, shooting a large hole in the second-storey galley not ten feet above Marcus's head.

"Give me that!" Gabrielle bolted to her feet and jerked the shotgun from Angus's hands.

"Excellent plan," Nick said with a smile at Gabrielle.

"By the way, Nick," Hale said, "I'm sure someone can take you to shore now. Thanks for stopping by and—"

"Hale," Kat said, cutting him off. "We need him."

"To do what, exactly?" Gabrielle wanted to know.

"Maggie," Kat said softly. "Someone's got to keep an eye on Maggie." She stood and walked tenderly to the rail. The coastline didn't seem so distant, but the details were still clouded in a fog. So she stared out at the water and tried to focus on the few things she truly knew. "We need to know where she goes, whom she talks to. If she buys anything, I want to hear about it. If she makes any calls, I want to know to whom and for how long."

"OK, OK. I got it." Nick plopped a grape into his mouth and turned for the door, but Hale was already up and blocking his way.

"I don't think you do."

"She's not just some old woman," Kat said, taking her place at Hale's side. "She's not a mark or a chump. She's been on the grift longer than any of us have been alive."

Nick laughed a little. "I seem to remember another lifelong con I managed to successfully tail one day in Paris."

"I mean it, Nick. She's good."

"So were you."

"I'm serious," Kat warned.

Nick wasn't smiling when he finished, "So am I." Then he stepped around Hale and went inside, leaving the crew to watch him go.

The Bagshaws had stopped shooting. Simon wasn't fiddling with any wires or keys. Even Gabrielle sat perfectly still, back straight, when she asked, "What are *we* going to do?"

"Simon, I want you to stay with the Interpol files. If there's something in there about Maggie, I want to know what it is. Angus, you and Hamish stay with LaFont. I want to know if he's in on it or if…"

Kat trailed off, leaving Hale to guess, "If she's using him like she used us?"

"Yes," Kat admitted.

"So what about us?" Gabrielle asked from under the brim of her hat.

"It sounds like the Cleopatra is taking over the town, right, Simon?" Kat asked.

"Right," Simon said.

Kat allowed herself one last look out across the blue water and the distant coast. "Then I think it's time we see the sights."

Fortress was a word that, in Katarina Bishop's opinion, was severely overused and overrated. It does not, for example, adequately describe a jewellery store or most banks. It is a serious misnomer for the vast majority of domestic military bases (with the obvious exception of Fort Knox). Even half of the royal residences in the world would not be best described in such a way. But not, Kat knew, in Monaco.

"You know, Marcus would have driven," Hale said as the two of them followed Gabrielle up the long winding road that led to the palace walls of the Grimaldi family home.

"Teens today don't get enough exercise, or haven't you heard?" Kat said, reaching to pat Hale's nonexistent gut.

What she found were flat, hard abs, and her face blushed a little.

"You know, about a half dozen armies have tried to take this place over the years," Hale said, huffing slightly as Gabrielle picked up the pace and the cobblestone street grew even steeper.

"Well then, it's a good thing we aren't an army, isn't it?" Gabrielle said.

The wind was clear and almost cool as it blew from the Mediterranean up through the cypress trees that lined the winding road.

"So if the ball is Thursday night, and they're auctioning it off at the palace on Friday..." Hale started.

Kat pointed to the tall walls in the distance. "Then the Prince's Palace is our last shot – which is a bad thing. Though it gives us the most prep time. Which is a good thing. But it's the palace..."

"Which is a bad thing?" Hale guessed, and smiled in her direction. For a split second, Kat almost forgot about the curse and the stone and what she was starting to think of as the most awkward kiss in the history of awkward kisses.

She pulled her camera from her pocket and scanned the bay below with its acres of yachts and motorboats. The palace sat atop a massive plateau that surged out into the water, raised that much closer to heaven by the rocky cliffs.

Gabrielle crossed her arms and stared out at the jagged limestone wall that rose up from the breaking waves. "I could totally scale that."

"Those cliffs are a hundred and fifty feet tall and eighty degrees steep," Kat said, with barely a glance in her cousin's direction.

Gabrielle was insulted and didn't even bother to hide it. "Oh, and I suppose you think your dad was alone when he free-climbed the Kyoto Banking Tower on a windy day last September."

"Cliffs mean many, many chances to fall, Gabrielle."

"So?" Gabrielle countered.

"So catch," Kat said, tossing a coin underhanded, sending it hurtling through the air in her cousin's direction. Gabrielle lunged to catch it, but her ankle turned and as she fell her purse toppled open, sending two wallets, three IDs, two bottles of fingernail polish, and a stun gun skidding across the cobblestones.

"Ow," Gabrielle said, then looked up at her cousin. "What did you do that for?"

Hale bent down, put a hand under each of Gabrielle's arms, and pulled her effortlessly to her feet.

"No cliffs," Kat said a final time.

Gabrielle sighed and admitted, "No cliffs."

Kat stood with one hand over her eyes blocking out the sun, staring at the stronghold in the distance. "So we can't go over, and it's sitting on solid stone, which means we can't go under. But if we get through –" she eyed the gates – "we'd still have to get to the stone and get it out..." She turned and looked at them. "We have to get *out*."

"Maybe Charlie could make another fake?" Hale suggested,

but Kat shook her head.

"No time."

"Maybe..." Gabrielle started, but Kat had already turned.

Gravity seemed stronger than normal, pulling Kat down the hill and over the cobblestone streets towards the sandy beaches below.

"What else does the emerald have planned, Hale?"

"You're not gonna like it," he said with a shake of his head, and Kat kept walking. She didn't like any of it.

Over the next five hours, Kat and her companions looked like most tourists who come to the French Riviera on any given year. But looks can be deceiving.

Standing outside La Banque Royale Nationale, very few of the passers-by could hear the shorter girl say to the boy, "LaFont's safe-deposit box is a part of the bank's platinum package?"

"Yeah."

"And the stone is being kept here whenever it isn't making official appearances?"

"Yes."

"And our last shot at it here would be Thursday night?"

The boy nodded. "Before the auction Friday morning."

"And don't tell me –" the girl pointed to the cameras that hung at regular intervals around the perimeter – "those are the Decanter 940s with the heat-sensitive imaging?"

"Yes," her companions answered in unison.

The girl slid a pair of dark sunglasses from the top of her

head and pulled them over her bright blue eyes. She didn't look back as she said, "Next."

Walking through the front doors of the Cathedral of Monaco, Kat had to look around.

"What is going to happen here?" she asked.

"Publicity photos," Hale said.

"OK..." Kat glanced at the doors and the cameras, the places where she could imagine the guards and the stone. "This could actually work if we get the right—"

"*With* the Palace Guards..." Hale added, and Kat turned on her heel and started for the door.

"Next!"

Standing outside the hotel suite where Maggie was set to host an afternoon tea for a visiting delegation of Egyptian dignitaries, Kat had an all-too-familiar reaction. (Too many hired goons, too few exits.)

The scene was no different on the street corner where, according to Simon, it might be possible to delay the armoured car for five additional minutes as the stone made its way to or from the Prince's Palace. (But there were too many bystanders and too little cover.)

There was a point somewhere between the bank and the royal jeweller's, where the gem would receive its official polishing, when the group allowed themselves a little hope; but soon Kat was shaking her head and walking away from that possibility, too (entirely too little time to prep, and besides, no crew under a curse should even consider a job requiring scuba gear).

So it was with a heavy heart and very low expectations that Kat turned to Hale. "And that leaves Thursday night..."

They had walked off the main thoroughfare. Simon was somewhere scanning the Interpol files, and Nick was still tailing Maggie. Marcus had appeared in a limo as if by magic and carried Gabrielle away. The Bagshaws were on the other side of the city, scouting LaFont's private home. So Kat and Hale were alone as they turned onto a small winding street lined with elegant boutiques and expensive sports cars.

"Do they have a location for the ball yet?"

"They do."

"Do we want to head over there now, or—"

"First, we make a stop." Hale turned towards a long glass window with a blue awning. The door chimed as he strolled inside.

Kat knew there was a trick – there had to be. Maybe the bank backed up to the store and the vault could be accessed via the basement. Maybe Maggie's stylist worked there and it would be possible for Gabrielle to impersonate her, switch the stones, and then escape in a trunk filled with couture.

Kat's mind was reeling in a way that young girls' minds almost never reel when inside elite boutiques on the coast of the Riviera. She was so busy, in fact, that she almost didn't see the salesgirl who was approaching Hale, smiling.

"I'm sorry," Kat told the girl. "We're not really shopping for—"

"Welcome back, Mr Hale," the girl gushed, and kissed Hale on each cheek as if Kat hadn't spoken at all. "I believe we have..." She trailed off, glancing at an equally tall, equally tan, equally gorgeous girl who was carrying a least a dozen bags from the back room.

"Yes, we have some beautiful things for you, Hale," the second girl said, handing him the bags, her hand lingering a little longer than necessary on his.

"You always do, Isabella. My love to Renée, OK?"

"*Bonjour*," Isabella said.

"*Bonjour*," Hale said back. They were halfway to the door when he finally looked at Kat. "*Now* we're ready."

Kat tested the weight and feel of the garment bag he'd handed her. "I don't suppose there's a heat-resistant black catsuit in here with built-in harness attachments?"

"Nope."

"Then I don't suppose you're going to tell me what is in here?"

Hale's smile was his only answer.

"I don't really have a big need for fancy dresses," Kat tried again.

"Tonight you do."

"Why? What's tonight? Where are we going?"

He stopped and slipped on his dark glasses. "My world."

TWENTY-SIX

Although the seasickness should, technically, have been waning, Kat felt more nauseous than usual when they finally made it back onboard the *W. W. Hale.* She tried to blame it on the changing weather, the shifting tides. She tried to tell herself that it was just a scouting trip – nothing more – but every time she caught sight of the garment bag lying on the end of the king-size bed, the feeling in her gut grew stronger, saying something was very, very wrong.

"Hey, Kitty," Gabrielle called, sidling into the room. "Angus and Hamish say the roads around the bank are a nightmare, so if we hit it there we're going to need a chopper or a..." She stopped suddenly and lunged for the garment bag. "Oh! I love this store!" she exclaimed, knocking a lamp off the bedside table and spilling a glass of juice before finally managing to rip open the bag.

"Oh," Gabrielle said, staring down. "It's *your* size." Curse or not, she still looked to Kat like a goddess as she held the gown against her body and studied her reflection in one of the stateroom's floor-length mirrors.

"Gabrielle." Kat's voice sounded small and timid. She barely recognised the sound, but given that they were the only two people in the room, she knew she must have been the one who'd spoken. She also knew that it was far too late to go back.

"Gabrielle," Kat said, stronger this time. She pulled the dress from her cousin's hands.

"What's wrong with you?" Gabrielle asked.

Kat wanted to talk about curses and emeralds and pride. Part of her wanted to scream about old cons and new cons and the perverse, twisted irony that comes with finally being *the mark*. But all that came out was "I kissed Hale".

"You did *what*? When? How?"

"I kissed Hale. After the heist. The usual way...I guess." She watched her cousin pick up the dress again and turn back to the mirror. Wordless. "Gabrielle?" The impatience was rising in Kat's voice. "Gabrielle, would you please put the dress down and—"

"I'm impressed, Kitty," Gabrielle said. "I was beginning to think you'd never take that plunge. So, how was it?"

"He *left*," Kat said, the memory rushing back. "I kissed him and he went to Uruguay."

"Paraguay," Gabrielle corrected. "And technically he never made it out of the country."

"He left," Kat said again, settling on the only thing that mattered.

"He's back now," Gabrielle countered.

But Kat's mind was already drifting, remembering every

touch – every smile. She pulled a silk-covered pillow onto her lap, longing for her mother's small bed in the pink room of Uncle Eddie's brownstone.

"He's mad at me."

"Um...I believe I said that several days and a couple thousand miles ago," Gabrielle said.

"I don't even know why."

Gabrielle spun on her good foot and eyed Kat. She tossed the designer dress onto the bed and said, "Of course you do."

"He doesn't like it when I take chances," Kat said. "But I really didn't *need* help with those jobs, Gabrielle. I wasn't in that much danger, and if I'd needed help I would have..." She trailed off, studying her cousin's expression. "What is it?"

"Nothing," Gabrielle said with a shrug. "It's just...did you ever think that maybe *needing* help and *wanting* Hale are two totally different things?"

Kat was the planner – the thinker – but she sat there for a long time, considering the possibility that Gabrielle might be the smartest girl in the world. Or, at least, in their world.

"Hale's my best friend," she said simply.

"I know."

"I'm not sure what would happen if he became my *boy*-friend."

"I know," Gabrielle said, as if she were happy that Kat was finally catching up.

The waves beat softly against the side of the yacht, and Kat felt her stomach turn as she thought about the one question she was almost afraid to ask.

"Do boys always go crazy when you kiss them?"

"Yes," Gabrielle said simply. "But not in the way that you're asking."

Kat might have asked exactly what her cousin meant, but there were too many mysteries in her life – too many vaults she couldn't crack – and only one that came with a ticking clock, so she reached for the gown.

"Gab, can you help me with—"

But Kat couldn't finish because the door flew open, and she jumped.

"Jeez, Simon," she said to the boy who stood panting in the hall outside. "You scared me half to... What's wrong?"

He looked from Kat to Gabrielle, then back again. His shirt was wrinkled and untucked. He looked like anything but a genius when he said, "Uh...I think you're both going to want to see this."

There was a room on the ship that Kat had never seen before. Situated on the top level near the bridge, it had plush couches and a grand piano. There were windows on three sides, and in the distance, she saw the sun setting over the sea. Despite the computers and trays covered with empty Coke cans and half-eaten sandwiches, it felt like a room made for champagne and caviar – maybe because of the view, Kat surmised. Or maybe because Hale was already there, and he was wearing a tuxedo.

"Hubba-hubba," Gabrielle told him, straightening his tie. But Kat couldn't take her gaze away from Simon.

"Tell me," she said.

"Well." Simon's voice was scratchy and breaking. He seemed almost afraid to say, "I was going through the files like you asked..."

"And you found Maggie, did you?" Angus said, when he and Hamish appeared in the door.

"Oh, no." Simon shook his head. His eyes were wide. "She doesn't have a file. I mean, there's nothing about Maggie in the database. As far as I can tell, she's not even on Interpol's radar. She might as well not even exist. She's—"

"Simon," Hale said, bringing him back.

"Right," Simon said with a quick point in Hale's direction. Then he turned back to Kat. "Like I said, I couldn't find her in the files. So I stopped looking for her."

"OK," Kat said, knowing this was important – that this mattered – she just couldn't yet imagine why.

"So instead I started looking...for *it*." Simon moved to the dusty file box Kat herself had carried out of Interpol's basement. "According to our friends in Lyon, there have been at least ten attempts to steal the Cleopatra since it was discovered. Paris in '49," he said, pulling a file from the box and dropping it onto the table. "Mexico City in '52. London in '63."

Simon seemed tired as he spoke, like the files and the secrets were wearing on him and taking their toll. Then he reached for the last one.

"And, of course, once at the World's Fair in Montreal."

"When?" Hale asked, but Kat's mind was going back

to another room and another night, and she thought about the keys she'd found during her crazy search of Uncle Eddie's office.

Her voice was barely more than a whisper. "Nineteen-sixty-seven."

Simon nodded slowly. "It was the first time the stone had ever been displayed for the general public and...well...it was a really big deal. *This* was taken on the opening night."

When he pushed a button on his computer, the whole crew watched as the screen filled with a black-and-white photograph of men in tuxedoes and ladies in gowns. The women wore their hair piled into elaborate updos. Thick liner trailed away from the corners of their eyes as if they were all channelling Cleopatra herself, but there was only one woman in the crowd who really mattered.

Simon pointed to a woman who was young and smiling and beautiful, and even decades and half a world away, there was no mistaking the woman they knew as Maggie. "That's her. Isn't it?"

"Yeah," Hale said. "That's her."

Kat felt suddenly as if she were snooping, prying, looking in on something she wasn't supposed to see – somewhere she didn't belong. But she couldn't turn away. Not then. They'd travelled too far and the stakes were too high. And she was in far too deep to do anything but stare at the corner of the photograph and the two identical faces that stared back.

Simon pointed at the brothers. "And she wasn't alone."

TWENTY-SEVEN

Kat vaguely remembered getting dressed. She was sure there was a conversation involving Gabrielle, the curse, and a wayward curling iron. (There also was a brief appearance by Marcus and a first-aid kit.) But the whole process of preparing for their scouting trip was really more of a blur to Kat, and even as she sat beside Hale in the small motorboat shuttling them from yacht to shore, she really could do nothing but stare out at the dark waves and whisper, "They looked so young. Didn't they look young?"

"Yeah," Hale said. "They did."

She wasn't a fool. She knew that her uncles had been young men once, tall and handsome. She'd heard the stories. She knew the legends. But looking at them in the prime of the con and the prime of their lives – seeing them together – was one of the strangest feelings that Kat had ever known.

She thought about Uncle Eddie and wanted to know what his plan had been, how the greatest thief she'd ever known had tried to steal the stone she'd chased halfway around the world. But more important, Kat wanted to know where it had all gone wrong.

She wondered what Uncle Eddie would tell the young men in that photo if he could go back in time and send them a message. Then she realised that maybe it was the same warning he'd been trying to give her.

"Maybe it was a coincidence – Maggie's being in that picture," Hale said. Kat looked at him. "OK. So maybe coincidence isn't the right word. But it was a big party – there were lots of people there."

"No." Kat shook her head and watched the boat pull into the dock. "She was part of it."

"How do you know?"

Because theirs wasn't a world of coincidence... Because Maggie had been chasing that stone for years... "Because I know her," Kat said finally. She couldn't look at him. "I know her, Hale. I think...I think I am her."

"No." Hale climbed from the boat and reached down, picked her up and onto the dock in one easy motion, held her tight. "You aren't."

TWENTY-EIGHT

To say Monaco is small would be something of an understatement. With just over thirty thousand people, it is roughly the size of New York's Central Park. Its resources are few and the opportunities for self-survival are limited, and yet somehow that rocky coast has become one of the wealthiest pieces of land on earth. So Kat walked along the cobblestone streets, Hale at her side, telling herself that anything was possible.

Well...almost anything.

"So here we are..." he said, pointing across the meticulously maintained gardens and fountains to the building that stood at the very heart of Monte Carlo.

"The Casino de Monte-Carlo," Kat said flatly. "You expect us to rob a casino."

"Rob *at* a casino," Hale hastened to add. "There's a difference. Besides –" he pointed to a banner in the distance, telling all the world that the Antony was on its way – "this is the last stop on the emerald's itinerary before Maggie auctions it off at the palace Friday morning." He offered his arm.

"So what do you say? You ready to case a casino?"

Kat looked at Hale, and at last her stomach didn't sway. She finally felt steady on her feet when she took his arm. "I'm ready to get the Cleopatra back."

Even though Kat had only known Hale for a little more than two years, she had seen him in a lot of situations. There was a long weekend in Brazil during Carnival. She had a very vivid recollection of a job involving ducks, helium and a steamship on its way to Singapore. It had occurred to her somewhere along the way that she had never – not once – seen him look out of place, but as they strolled onto the main casino floor, there in the heart of Monte Carlo, Kat couldn't help but think that she'd never seen him truly at home, either.

Then she watched the way he pulled a leather wallet from the inside pocket of his perfectly tailored tuxedo jacket and told the elderly gentleman working behind the bars at the window, "Change five hundred, please."

The gesture was so easy, the voice so confident, that the man in the booth never even asked to see an ID, and Kat knew that this was as close to home as W. W. Hale the Fifth might ever come.

"What?" he asked, right before Kat realisd she was staring. He gave her a wide-mouthed grin. "Do I have something in my teeth?"

"Yes." She smirked. "I think the canary left some feathers in there after you ate it."

The attendant slid a golden ticket through the slot in the

cage, and Hale placed it into his coat pocket, patting the place over his heart for extra measure.

"Come on." Hale took her hand. "I feel lucky."

That might have been a good time to remind him about the curse. It might have been an equally appropriate time to point out that blackjack was a game of probability, and roulette belonged to fools – all the little things that she had learned at her father's knee and Uncle Eddie's kitchen table.

So, no, luck had nothing to do with anything, as far as Kat was concerned, but right then did not seem like the proper time to say so, because Hale put her right hand in his own and placed his left gently at her waist, guiding her through the tall doors and the crowd. Kat couldn't help but think that it was almost like a homecoming dance. Or maybe a prom. For one brief moment, she allowed herself to feel like a normal girl, all dressed up and on the town with the boy of her dreams. But then they stopped at an ornate railing and looked across the casino floor. It stretched out beneath them, roulette wheels spinning. Cards flipping. Tuxedoed men and elegant women almost as far as the eye could see. And Kat knew that nothing about her life was ever going to be normal.

"So this is where the ball will be..." Kat said.

"Our last shot before the auction," Hale went on. He leaned onto the rail and turned to look at her. "So how's it look?"

Kat wanted to say beautiful. Most would have said glamorous. It was easy to imagine the room full of big bidders and music and food and, of course, the most valuable emerald

228

that the world had ever known, so Kat just shook her head and said, "Hard."

Hale looked at her. "You know, I've always loved a good party."

Kat let her gaze drift across the room and knew that a sane person would have experienced a small bit of panic when she counted the guards (28 on the main floor, 56 in total). Uncle Eddie, by all rights, could have disinherited her for not walking away as soon as she counted the steps from the emerald's likely position to the nearest exit (212).

There were too many thoughts inside her head in that moment – too many theories and strategies and plans. Kat closed her eyes and cleared her mind. What would Visily Romani do? she wondered for a split second, then shook her head and asked the question that had been plaguing her for hours: what *did* Uncle Eddie do? And Charlie? And Maggie?

Maggie...

"Well, of course they're giving me a line of credit!" a big brassy voice yelled from down below. "A great big green one!" Maggie finished, and the crowd that surrounded her erupted into laughter. But, to Kat, nothing was funny any more.

The ornate railing was smooth beneath her palms as she stood staring down at Maggie, who laughed and talked and cajoled like the queen of the ball.

Maggie, who had sat trembling in that rainy diner, holding a black-and-white photo of someone else's childhood and begging someone else's child to take a terrible chance.

Maggie, who had used the name Romani.

Maggie, who had stood in a room much like that with Kat's uncles in 1967, and had been chasing that emerald ever since.

My uncles, Kat thought to herself, then smiled sadly. Her uncles would know what to do.

Then, with the thought, her smile changed.

"What are you looking at?" Hale asked. "Why are you smiling? I worry when you smile."

"I know why she did it, Hale. I know why she conned me."

"Well...yeah," Hale said. "I can think of a hundred million reasons."

"No, Hale." Kat pressed her hands against his chest, felt his heart pounding beneath her palms as she said, "I know why she conned *me*. You can't pull this job without the real thing – forty years ago maybe, if the fake was really good and the black market really shady. But you can't even do a black market deal with today's technology. And if you don't have the real Antony...and if you can't fake the Antony..."

"You can't *sell* the Antony," Hale finished for her.

Kat nodded and shrugged. "So the only way to *pretend* you have the Antony is if you really do have the Cleopatra. And the only way to pass off the Cleopatra as the Antony is if you know where there's a *fake* Cleopatra to swap it for. But how many forgers in the world can do that?"

"Just Charlie?" Hale guessed.

Kat nodded and sighed. "Just Charlie."

She turned slowly around, her gaze sweeping over the room – tuxedos and ball gowns and the place where the emerald would soon be holding court at the centre of the party. It was almost as if the world turned to black-and-white and it was 1967 all over again. Kat didn't dare think what it would feel like to chase that stone for fifty more years.

"Here," Kat said beneath the din of the crowd. "We do it here."

"Um, Kat, not to be a spoilsport, but you did see the guards, didn't you?" Hale asked.

"Yes," she said, and for some reason, she couldn't hold back a laugh.

"And that number is going to go up by...say...twenty per cent once they get the stone in here?"

"More like thirty," she corrected. "If we're lucky. But it has to be here, Hale." She thought of her uncles: handsome, young, identical. A genetic sleight of hand. "We can do it here if we can get help – if we can get someone inside."

"OK. I can—"

"Not you."

Hale hung his head, but eventually admitted, "Fine, then Nick..."

But he trailed off when Kat turned to him and smiled as if she'd temporarily forgotten what it felt like to be the mark.

"We're not the only ones who are going to have to trust him," she said with a shake of her head. "Which means we're going to need *the* inside man."

Hale took a tentative step back and studied her. "So..."

"So how do you feel about helicopters?"

3 DAYS UNTIL
THE AUCTION

SOMEWHERE IN
AUSTRIA

TWENTY-NINE

"Hello, Uncle Charlie."

Kat and Hale stood with their hands in their pockets, shivering inside too-thin coats while the snow swirled around them. A storm was coming. The wind was colder than she'd remembered. Or maybe, Kat thought, it was just the look in her great-uncle's eyes as he said, "You have a lot of nerve, bringing your trouble to my mountain."

He pushed away from the door and moved through the dim house, sidestepping urns and canvases and furniture, calling behind him, "Go to your uncle, Katarina."

"I *am* with my uncle."

"Edward would—"

"Eddie's on the other side of the world, Uncle Charlie. Eddie doesn't care—"

Charlie stopped and spun. "He'd care about *this*."

"Why?" she asked, easing closer to the place where he stood, a poker in his hand, staring down at the fire. "Why does the Cleopatra Emerald matter so much, Uncle Charlie? What happened in 1967?"

"We do not talk about that, Katarina."

"Fine. Then let's talk about *her*."

Kat had torn a picture from a newspaper, and she pulled it from her pocket, the headline screaming out in French.

"She's calling herself Maggie now. A few weeks ago she said her name was Constance Miller and that Visily Romani wanted me to steal the Cleopatra Emerald. She's a con artist, Uncle Charlie. A great one." She studied her uncle's face, watched his breath stay even and slow, with not a single telltale sign of recognition. "But you already knew that, didn't you?"

Charlie shook his head and gestured towards the tiny cluttered room. "I'm afraid my circle of friends is not as big as it used to be. I'm sorry I can't help." The words sounded right, but it was like watching an athlete who's been away from the game. He was rusty and slow, but the talent was still there, oozing underneath.

"Nice try, Charlie." Kat smiled. "The timing was right, but your eyes –" she pointed to her own dark lashes – "they're a little out of practice."

"Kat—"

"She conned me, Uncle Charlie. She is so good, and I was...cocky." Kat laughed even though she knew it wasn't funny – not funny at all. "She told me exactly what I wanted to hear." She risked a glance at Hale, waited for him to nod before she went on. "So we did what no crew has ever done before. We stole the Cleopatra Emerald."

In the stillness of the room, only the cracking and popping

of the fire made a sound. She wasn't expecting Charlie to tell her it was OK. She had no hopes of comfort. Only truth.

"I got conned," Kat admitted. "And for a long time I couldn't see why. Why take the risk of angering Uncle Eddie and my dad and a whole bunch of people who are really good at revenge? Why use *me* when there are a half-dozen crews who are just as good?"

"I don't know her," he said again.

"Yes you do, Charlie," Kat told him. "Because the only way to pass the Cleopatra off as the Antony is if no one knows the Cleopatra is gone. The only way to run the con she's running is if you have a *fake* Cleopatra. And the only person who can fake the Cleopatra is you."

"I don't know her, Katarina."

"Yes." Kat reached into her pocket and found the second photo – the one with ball gowns and tuxedos, really big hairdos, and an emerald at the centre of the fair. "You do."

Charlie's hands didn't shake when he reached for it. He stood by the mantel for a long time, staring down. "She got old," he said softly, then in a flash, the picture was in the fire, dissolving in the flames. "But I guess she's not the only one."

Not for the first time, Kat wondered what had happened to Charlie, what made him stay at the top of that mountain, trapped inside the snow and the wind, hidden from his family and his world. Kat let herself wonder if Uncle Eddie was right – if *she* was still running – and maybe bound for a mountain of her own someday.

"What happened in '67, Uncle Charlie?"

237

"Jobs go bad, Kat. You know that." He tried to move away, but Kat grabbed his hand, held on for dear life.

"Bad enough to scare Uncle Eddie? To drive the two of you apart?" She gripped his fingers, stared into his eyes. "What happened in '67?"

Charlie tried to pull away. "Ask your uncle."

"I *am*," she countered. "Whoever Maggie is, she used the name Romani. She used me. And you. She used us," Kat said, pleading, but Charlie only laughed.

His eyes were dark, joyless, when he whispered, "It's not the first time."

Kat watched her uncle ease into the chair by the fire and take a deep breath. He seemed years older when he said, "In 1959, two brothers left Romania and struck out on their own. They made their way across Eastern Europe and the Baltics – London for a time. And along the way, they met a girl..."

Kat took her place on a footstool, felt the heat of the fire burning through the back of her legs, thawing her from the inside out. It was almost like being in Uncle Eddie's kitchen as she sat there, listening, learning, trying to understand more about their world.

"She changed us, Katarina. You wouldn't have recognised Eddie – or me," Charlie added with a laugh. "We were... drunk...on her. She was just the kind of woman it was hard not to love. Smart. Fearless. I never told anybody how I felt, but Eddie swore he was going to marry her. He even bought the ring. All he was waiting for was one big score to prove himself to her. *The* big score."

"Like the Cleopatra Emerald," Hale said.

Charlie nodded. "Exactly. The whole world was infatuated with that stone. Everyone said it was cursed, sure – but truth be told, that just made us want it more. All the best crews had tried for it – and failed. But the three of us...we didn't listen. We just watched and planned. And waited."

"Until the World's Fair?" Hale guessed. Charlie nodded.

"It had never been shown in public before, so I went to work on the fake. Eddie played inside. And she..." He trailed off. "Well, she played everyone."

"What happened?" Kat said.

"Eddie planned it so that I could make the switch and get the real stone out, but she said I should give it to her instead – that she'd take the stone to Eddie and tell him...tell him that she and I were in love. She said we'd let him keep the Cleopatra to soften the blow. And then she and I would be free to be together." Charlie looked down at the fire. "You were right, Katarina. She is good."

"So you changed the plan," Kat said, finally starting to understand. "Is that where the job went bad?"

"Honestly?" Charlie raised an eyebrow. "No. She'd thought of everything. It would have worked, but a guard messed up...a fluke thing. He left a window open and a bird flew in, set off all the sensors – brought an army down on us. Eddie and I barely made it out alive. That's when we learned she'd planned on taking the stone and running away from us both. Brothers. She was willing to come between brothers." Charlie sighed. "And we let her. So don't feel bad, Katarina. As far as marks go, you are in excellent company."

Hale was moving forward, leaning close. "In three days she's going to sell the Cleopatra – pass it off as the Antony."

"Of course she is." Charlie reached out to stoke the fire, sparks and embers flaring. "That was the original plan."

"But we can get it back," Kat heard herself confiding.

"It won't work." Charlie shook his head in the manner of someone who has lived and learned and is content never to make the same mistakes again.

"It *will* work," Kat said. "It will work if we have you."

"I can't make another stone like that. Not in three days." He ran a varnish-stained hand across his scruffy face. "Not ever."

Kat shook her head. "I don't need a stone, Charlie. I need a con."

"No. No," he said, and his gaze flew to the door, as if there were something lurking outside, beating against the side of the house like the snow and the wind, fighting to get in.

"Yes, Charlie." She reached for his hand. "I've been trying for days to think of someone she doesn't know – someone we can trust to work inside. But then I realised that someone she knows is the *perfect* person."

"Eddie. You want Eddie."

She would have given anything to tell him he was wrong, but Eddie was the master, the best. He was also on the other side of the world and the other side of a line that said no one steals the Cleopatra Emerald, so Kat shook her head and stared up at the next best thing.

"Uncle Eddie can't... No, Uncle Eddie *won't* help me, Charlie. Not this time. This time I need you."

"I loved her, Katarina." Heartbreak seeped into his eyes. It seemed to take him a moment to realise what he'd said. "And so did he."

When Charlie pulled away, the best hands in the business were shaking. His lip quivered. And Kat hated herself for bringing that darkness to his door.

"I'm sorry, Charlie." She hesitated for a moment but then leaned down and kissed his head. She started for the door. "I won't bother you any more."

"Margaret Gray."

Kat stopped and turned. She watched him run a hand through his hair in a gesture she'd seen his brother make a thousand times.

"Her name is Margaret Gray," he said slowly. "And I never want to see her again."

THIRTY

It was almost dusk by the time the small motorboat made it back to the *W. W. Hale*. It said a great deal about Kat's current state of mind that she really didn't want to crawl aboard the larger, safer vessel.

"Maybe I could just sit here for...a week or two," she told Hale.

"Not this time," he said, grabbing her hand and pulling her on board.

Marcus stood ten feet away, posture perfectly straight, a tray of tea and scones in his hands.

Simon had covered the ship's massive windows with figures and formulas, and he pointed between them and Gabrielle. Ordinarily, this would have been a source of very little concern, except that Gabrielle was wearing high heels and a rappelling harness and arguing.

"Kat!" Simon threw up his hands in disgust and walked towards her. "Will you tell your cousin the kind of damage falling from over a hundred feet can do?"

On the deck above, the Bagshaws were yelling something

about old wiring systems and backup generators, neither bothering to remove their protective headphones, so they just yelled louder.

"Why don't you just ask Kat?" Hamish yelled.

"Yeah," his brother countered. "Be that way and I'll ask Kat!"

"Guys," Gabrielle said, but the word was lost amid the smoke and the headphones. "Guys!" she tried again. "Kat's here!"

Hamish was oblivious as he turned and pointed. "Hey, Kat's here."

It was Nick alone who looked from Kat to the way Hale leaned against the rail with his arms crossed. It might have been a perfectly adequate poker face anywhere else in the world, but it wasn't quite good enough for Monte Carlo.

So Nick stepped closer to Kat and asked, "Where were you?"

"Austria," Hale answered, but Nick acted like he hadn't even heard.

"You fly off in the middle of the night, leaving nothing but a shopping list and an *I'll be back*. So where were you?" Nick wanted to know.

"Austria," Kat said, as if Hale's answer should have been good enough.

"You know how to do it, don't you, Kitty?" Hamish was practically out of breath from his run down the stairs when he bolted onto the deck before her.

"So what is it?" Angus asked, appearing at his brother's

side and rubbing his hands together. In the dim light, his eyes seemed to glow. "Is it Hansel and Gretel?"

"Can't be," Hamish told him. "We only have the one grenade launcher."

"Right." Angus nodded as if Hamish had a most excellent point.

"That's not it, guys," Hale said with a quick shake of his head.

But Nick was stepping closer to Kat. The words, she could tell, were meant only for her. "What was in Austria?"

Kat no longer felt the rock and sway of the ship, but she was far from steady on her feet as she told him, "Our exit strategy." She pushed past them. "He said no."

She'd hoped that would be the end of it, but then she saw the way the deck was lined with cord and cable, a feather boa, two ball gowns, three tuxes, a box with a French label citing that the contents were extremely explosive, and at least six dozen long-stemmed roses (which Kat had yet to decide whether or not they should even try to use).

"Kat," Simon spoke softly, "what happened?"

Kat looked across the faces that stared back at her, open and tired and confused, and she knew it was too late. For everything.

"I thought I had a way, guys. I really did. But Uncle Eddie was right – no one steals the Cleopatra Emerald. I'm sorry I conned you all into thinking that we could do it twice."

Every decent con man knows that the simplest truth is more powerful than even the most elaborate lie. Kat saw it then. It broke against them all like the waves.

"So we get another plan," Gabrielle said.

"What about the bank?" Simon asked. "We've got the Bagshaws..."

"While we appreciate the vote of confidence, my boy," Hamish said with a slap on Simon's back, "it's a vault thirty feet beneath the priciest real estate in the world."

"So no?" Simon said.

Hamish shook his head. "No."

"Does she know the Wind in the Willows?" Gabrielle asked.

Angus looked at his brother. "I'm pretty sure she *was* the original Willow."

"Transit?" Hale asked.

"Yeah...um...no." Simon shook his head as if even the thought scared him. "LaFont was on his cell most of the day arranging for transportation."

"Armoured car?" Hale guessed.

"For starters," Simon said. "It seems the Palace Guards are also going to escort the truck. And there was talk of maybe a parade."

Hale spun back to Kat. "How do you feel about parades?" he asked.

"Hate them."

"You could ride on the back of a convertible," he teased.

"No, thank you."

"What if I throw in a sash? Gabrielle could teach you to wave, couldn't you, Gabs?" But Gabrielle was too busy changing the ice pack that was now a permanent feature on some part of her body to notice.

"Anne Boleyn?" Hamish suggested.

"No!" Hale and Kat cried in unison.

"Oscar the Grouch?" Gabrielle suggested.

"Does LaFont look to you like the kind of guy who takes out his own garbage?" Angus shot back, then shrugged. "Besides, he's not in on it. The best we can tell, he's getting conned just like everyone else."

It took a second for that knowledge to wash over them all, but then Gabrielle bolted upright, saying, "Ooh! I know!"

Kat cut her off with a wave. "The Prince's Palace is a fortress, Gabrielle."

"I know," Gabrielle said. "But palaces are fun."

"This one isn't. It's got a twenty-foot fence and a thirty-man rotating guard detail. And they're armed."

Even in the dim light, Kat could see Gabrielle beginning to pout. "Which wouldn't be a problem if you'd let me scale the cliffs."

"Wait." Hamish eased forward. "Why do we have to do it this week? We let ol' Maggie sell it, see? Then when it's all safe and sound in its new home..."

"There's no way of knowing where it's going," Hale said. "It could end up underground."

"In the private collection of some warlord or weapons dealer," was Gabrielle's guess.

Simon shook his head in frustration. "There are too many variables to account for the—"

"They might not be crooks." As soon as Kat blurted the words, she saw five sets of eyes turn to her, look at her like she was crazy. Only Nick seemed to understand.

"Not everyone's a bad guy," he told them. "We wait and do this job later, and *we* might be the bad guys."

"This is our window. Now." Kat stood back and paced. "We've got tomorrow morning..."

Hale shook his head. "No time. No access."

"The auction at the palace?"

"No good," Simon said. "*If* we get over the walls –" he gave a considerate look at Gabrielle – "no exit."

"OK." Kat took a deep breath. "That leaves us with..."

"The casino," Hale said flatly.

"You should tell someone, Kat." Nick's voice was cold but his eyes were warm. "My mom—"

"If you want to go home to Mommy, there's the door." Hale pointed over the side of the ship to the blue water and the long swim, but Nick ignored him.

He looked at Kat and asked, "How many cameras on the casino floor?"

"Sixty-two," she said, without missing a beat.

"How many entrances?" Nick went on.

"Five public, three private and four unofficial."

"Exits?"

"Ten."

"Average time to the street?"

"Two and a half minutes."

"Guards?"

"At least twenty on the floor. Four on the emerald."

"No." Nick was shaking his head. "Not even you can rob a casino, Kat."

"We're not robbing a casino, new boy." Hale pushed Nick aside.

"We're robbing *at* a casino," Gabrielle said with a smug smile. "There's a difference."

"Guys," Kat snapped, needing everyone to stop and think. "You're not listening. We can *get* the stone at the casino. But we can't get it *out*. Not without an inside man."

"I thought that was my job," Nick said.

Hale scoffed. "We need someone inside we can *trust*."

"Yeah –" Nick nodded – "because I came all this way for revenge."

But Kat was already shaking her head. "We need someone *she* will trust."

"I can make her trust *me*," Nick countered.

Kat thought about Maggie – a woman who had been on the grift and on her own for nearly half a century. "I don't think she's trusted anyone in a very long time."

"But you just said..." Nick started.

"I'm sorry, Nick. But you're the inside *boy*." Gabrielle's smile softened the blow. "I think what Kat's saying is we need the inside *man*." She turned back to her cousin. "Or at least I think that's what she's saying, since she hasn't even told us her plan."

"It's not my plan, Gabrielle," Kat said. "Or it isn't any more, since it won't work with who we've got."

Gabrielle crossed her arms. "Let us be the judge of that."

Kat felt everyone looking at her, staring, really. She felt her options dwindling down to one: tell them everything.

"Simon," she said, rolling up her sleeves, "we're gonna need those casino blueprints..."

2 DAYS UNTIL
THE AUCTION

THE W. W. HALE

THIRTY-ONE

Kat didn't mean to oversleep – she really didn't. But neither did she set an alarm or give Marcus a time to wake her. She didn't bother to open the curtains so that the sun would streak across her bed, and even when Gabrielle left the next morning, Kat didn't stir. When she heard the Bagshaws hitting golf balls into the sea, she didn't shush them. All she managed to do was toss and turn, one thought lapping against her subconscious over and over like a wave.

You cannot con an honest man.

So how did Maggie con me?

"Get up!"

"Hale," Kat said and rolled away. She heard him throw the curtains aside, saw bright light flooding the room. "I'm sleeping!" she yelled, and pulled the covers over her head.

"Get dressed." He jerked the blankets off the bed. Kat felt her short hair stand on end from the static, but Hale made no jokes, no quips. He just scavenged the floor for clothes.

"Here," he said, tossing an old sock and dirty T-shirt in her direction.

"Hale, I'm not— Ow!" she said, and rubbed the spot where a shoe ricocheted off her shoulder and hit her in the side of the head. But Hale hardly noticed because in the next second a leather miniskirt was flying towards her. "That's Gabrielle's," she told him.

"I don't care," he said, and started for the door. "You've got ten minutes."

"No, Hale. I can't...*think*...any more." Without realising it, Kat had risen to her knees. Beyond the windows, the Mediterranean stretched as far as the eye could see, but Kat felt trapped there. "I used to be able to see things. But now...I don't know how to do this, Hale. I don't. I can't get anyone caught or hurt or...

"I don't know how to do this," she repeated slowly.

"You said we need an exit strategy, right?"

"Right," she told him.

"So we're gonna go find an exit strategy." He stopped in the door. "Now you've got nine minutes."

Katarina Bishop was not a girl who liked to gamble. So, walking into the casino that afternoon, Kat didn't watch the tables. She didn't turn to the slots. And yet Kat couldn't shake the feeling that the odds were very long and the stakes were very high and that her luck almost certainly needed to hold.

She stood by the rail, looking out over the room that seemed entirely different in the light of day. Tourists had descended from cruise ships and now crowded around the tables in their flip-flops and floral shirts. Workmen scurried about with ladders and tool belts, setting the stage for the upcoming ball, all of them intent on turning the casino into a fortress.

Well, almost all of them.

"How's it going, Simon?" Kat asked, looking across the casino floor to the one workman who wore fake glasses and an equally fake beard and seemed to care more about blackjack than the task at hand.

"This guy is splitting tens," he said, and Kat wondered if he was really speaking to her at all. She doubted it.

"Simon!" Hale snapped, joining Kat at the rail. "I thought you didn't count cards."

"Counting isn't playing," he corrected, and went on about his business, leaving Kat to turn to the boy beside her.

"Hey," she told him.

"Hey, yourself," Hale said, gazing out over the massive room. "So, is the gang all here?"

"Hamish?" Kat spoke through her comms. "Angus? You ready?"

"Just waiting on the green light from Nicky, love," came Angus's reply.

"Nick?" Kat asked, but didn't glance around the room.

"I'm at the hair salon," Nick said. "Maggie just went in, so you're clear, Kat. Oh, and Angus, don't call me love. Or Nicky."

"Gabrielle?" Kat asked, and turned her gaze across the room. She couldn't see her cousin, but she heard her "Ready when you are" as clear as day. That left only one question.

"Are you sure we want to do this, Hale?"

He turned towards her slowly and winked. "Just try to stop us."

"OK." Kat took a deep breath and looked out over the railing. The most famous and luxurious casino in the world lay before her, preparing for the party of the century, but all Kat could do was shrug. And laugh. And tell Hamish, "Let 'em fly."

No one was certain how it happened. Later, people heard the rumour that five hundred white doves had gone missing from a wedding on the beach, but no one ever knew how the birds had made it out of their cages on the rocky shore and into one of the most exclusive casinos in the world.

The first thing anyone noticed was the noise, a rhythmic beating that might have got lost beneath the whirling of the roulette wheels and the yells of the tourists, had it not grown – louder and louder, closer and closer. And when the first of the birds broke into the casino's main floor, it was like the rushing of a flood.

There were cries and screams in a dozen languages. Women crawled under blackjack tables. Men lunged to protect their chips. Workmen appeared with brooms and mops as if to shoo the animals towards the doors, but birds – as any thief knows – always prefer to find their own way out.

The doves kept coming, filling the casino, landing among the cards and the chips and – above all – circling through the air, spiralling like smoke looking for the nearest exit.

Exits.

Chaos spread through the crowd, but Kat stood perfectly still, the scene in sharp focus like blueprints in her mind.

She saw the guards and the cameras, the skylights and heating ducts, service entrances and small crevices in the casino's defences, almost invisible to the naked eye – all while five hundred birds filled the air, looking for a way out, and Kat let them.

"Um...guys..." Nick sounded worried, but Kat wasn't really in a position to reply.

"We're kind of *busy* right now," Gabrielle told him. At the centre of the room, the banner announcing the Antony Ball was being dive-bombed by doves, and dangled, literally, by a thread.

"Well, you're about to get busier because Maggie's heading your way," Nick shouted. "And she's not alone. Looks like she's added a new guy to her posse."

Kat heard all this, of course, but the utilisation of five hundred doves to pinpoint the cracks (literally and otherwise) in a casino's defences is not something that can be redone, so Kat kept her eyes on the room, unwavering. Unyielding. It was her focus that made her lethal – like a laser, Uncle Felix had often teased. It was that focus that made her stupid, Uncle Eddie had one time warned.

And, as with most things, Kat would eventually come to realise, Uncle Eddie was exactly right.

She heard Hale shout, "Who?"

"I don't know," Nick told him. "I've never seen him before. Well dressed. Walking stick. Kinda regal and...old."

"Ha!" Despite the chaos, Kat heard Hamish laugh. "If I didn't know any better, Nicky my boy, I'd swear you were describing—"

"Uncle Eddie," Kat whispered. She stood stock-still at the top of the stairs, looking down at the small group of people that stood at the bottom, the only quiet in the chaos, looking up at her. "He's here."

"What is the meaning of this?" Pierre LaFont shouted at a casino employee, then turned to Maggie. "Madame, I give you my most sincere word that this will not impose upon the Antony Ball in any way."

"Oh," Maggie said slowly, still staring at the girl at the top of the stairs. "I hope not."

Kat knew even without looking that Simon was shrouded in the shadows of a massive potted plant. Hale was somewhere deep inside the room. Gabrielle was gone. The Bagshaws were with her. And Nick had no reason to darken the casino's doors, but none of that really mattered.

Maggie looked from the birds and the destruction and then back to Kat, and Kat knew that they were made – there was no place left to run. She started down the stairs, stepping over droppings and feathers. She didn't look at her uncle, but instead kept her eyes trained on the woman by his side.

"Hello, Maggie."

There was really nothing else for Maggie to do but turn to

the man beside her and say, "Monsieur LaFont, surely you remember my niece?"

The art dealer nodded. "Of course." He reached out to kiss her hand. "Mademoiselle, I am so sorry for this terrible... fiasco."

"Freak accident, I guess," Kat told him.

Maggie smiled. "Indeed."

"And, darling..." Maggie turned to Kat as if there were another introduction to be made, but before she could say another word, Kat's uncle placed his arm around Kat's shoulders.

"Hello again, Katarina." He squeezed tightly and turned her from the group. "We have so much to catch up on. Allow me to escort you home."

Kat didn't know how good the fresh air would feel until she breathed it. Outside, a cool wind was blowing off the Mediterranean. Doves perched in trees and left messes on the windshields of quarter-million-dollar cars, but none of that really mattered to Kat Bishop. She was too focused on the hand that gripped her waist, the stern voice that spoke low and in Russian, swearing at timing and curses and fate.

"Eddie!"

When she heard the scream, she stopped and turned to see Simon and the Bagshaws bursting through the doors.

"It's not her fault!" Angus cried.

"If you're gonna blame her, blame us," Hamish added.

But Kat...Kat kept looking at the man in front of her,

seeing past his dark overcoat and trimmed goatee to his eyes and mouth and hands.

"You have to—"

"Boys," Kat said, cutting Simon off. "I think it's time you met our uncle Charlie."

THIRTY-TWO

That afternoon as the *W. W. Hale* floated somewhere off the coast of Monaco, there was a feeling on the deck, something that mingled with the sun and the sea air. Kat breathed deeply and looked out across the water. She scarcely dared to call it hope.

"And that's the plan," she heard Hale tell the man who sat across from her, silent and still. "So what do you think, Charlie? Does that sound like something you can do?"

That was *the* question, really, and the whole crew sat waiting while the older man turned and stared into the distance. He looked like he was wondering what was out there and how much of a head start he might have.

"Charlie?" Gabrielle asked, and his head snapped back. "How does it sound?"

"Fine." He rubbed his hands on the tops of his thighs, warming them. "Fine. Fine. It's been a while, that's all."

"You'll do great," Hale said in the easy confident way that all great inside men are born with.

Charlie must have heard it too, because he raised his

eyebrows and said, "Don't con a conner."

Hale laughed. "Point taken." His voice was kind and soft and patient. "You're not going to have much time to do your job. But that's not a problem for you. You can do it. And when you do your job..."

"We can do our job and still get out of there alive," Gabrielle finished.

"You look just like..."

"Hamish!" Kat warned, stopping him just before he poked the old man in the side as if to see if he were real. "Perhaps we should give Uncle Charlie some *space*," she warned, watching the way her uncle leaned closer to the rail, preferring the company of the sea and a hundred miles of empty water.

The Bagshaws nodded slowly. "Sorry. It's just...it's an honour to finally meet you," Angus said.

"Yeah," Simon agreed.

Kat knew why they were staring. It was hard not to, to tell the truth. Charlie was part legend, part ghost, and sitting there in the warm sunshine with his hair trimmed and his face freshly shaved, he seemed a long, long way from his cold mountain.

No, Kat thought. He seemed like Uncle Eddie.

"You got the varnish off," Kat said.

"What?" he asked, jerking his head as if, for a second, he'd mentally escaped back to the safety of his cabin.

"Your hands – you got them clean." Kat reached to hold one, but Charlie pulled back, placed the hand in his pocket, and hissed, "I hope you kids know what you're doing."

"Don't worry, Charlie, my boy." Hamish gave an uncomfortable pat on the old man's back. "Perhaps you haven't heard, but a few months back ol' Kitty here put together a crew that—"

"This is no painting!" the man snapped, and pointed to the distant shore. "And *that* is no museum!" The eyes were so dark and the words so sharp, that for a second, Kat could have sworn she was looking at Uncle Eddie. Then the hands began to shake. The voice cracked. "And she is no mark."

"I know," Kat said, but her uncle talked on.

"The Cleopatra Emerald is—"

"Cursed – we know," Gabrielle said, touching the bruise on her shin.

"No." Her uncle shook his head. "It's not cursed. It just makes people *stupid*."

That was it, Kat realised. All the guilt and the shame boiled down to that. She'd been stupid. And that was something someone in her line of business could never afford to be.

"Forgive me, Katarina." Charlie rubbed a hand over his face, as if feeling for the beard – the man – he'd left behind in the snow. "It's just harder than I thought to watch history repeat itself."

"It won't be like last time, Charlie," Hale told him. "Maggie or Margaret or whatever her name is...we're out ahead of her this time."

"No one's ever been ahead of her," he said to the sea.

"I know," Kat told him. "But with your help, we will be.

Now that we have you, we can—"

Charlie rose, cutting her off. "Don't let two men fall in love with you, girls. It's not the sort of thing that ends well."

He walked towards Marcus and the small boat and the shore. And all Kat could do was sit there, her faith and hopes riding on his shoulders, and let him go.

Even after Charlie was gone, the ghost of the man still walked among them. A shadow on the floor. The wind across the deck. Night came and carried with it the promise of a new day, but no one slept. Kat walked through the halls but stopped short when she saw the play of light across the threshold of a partially cracked door. She crept towards it, peered inside at Nick, who sat straddling a cane chair, holding a deck of cards.

She knew the routine, had done it herself a million times, and still she stayed quiet, watching as he pulled the queen of spades from the deck with his right hand, held it tenderly on his palm and tapped it once with his left. The card was there, the gesture said. His hands flashed, a blur. The card was gone.

"You ready?"

To his credit, Nick didn't jump at the sound of her voice. "I will be." He looked up at her, then, as if from nowhere, he flashed the card again. "You?"

"As I'll ever be."

Kat still didn't like the water, but the solitude of the sea was something she could get used to. She stepped onto the deck, felt it when Nick followed, and savoured the sound of nothingness that surrounded them. The yacht drifted, motor silent. The crew was sound asleep. Even the waves seemed to be taking the night off, resting. Saving up their strength for the long day that lay ahead.

"So are you going to tell me how it happened?" Nick asked. "Exactly how did Katarina Bishop get conned into stealing the Cleopatra Emerald?"

"That depends," Kat answered. "Are you going to tell me why you really followed me here?"

He smiled. "You first."

Kat took a deep breath and looked up at the moon. It seemed bigger than it should have, closer. It was the kind of night where anything was almost possible, so she drew a deep breath and said, "Maggie or Constance or Margaret – whatever her name is – she said Romani sent her. She said it was rightfully hers and—"

"You believed her," Nick said, filling in the rest. He gave a long sigh. "You don't have to right all the wrongs of the world yourself, you know. I can put you in touch with people who do that for a living..."

"Somehow I don't think Interpol would be fooled by my fake ID." Kat thought about her trip to the Paris field office last fall, then added, "*Again.*"

"You don't have to do this, Kat."

"I've been hearing that a lot lately."

"He's right."

"I didn't say *who* had said it," she countered.

"You didn't exactly have to." He looked out at the water.

"You two are good together."

"We're not together," Kat said automatically.

"Sure you are. You just don't know it yet." He leaned against the rail. "And I'm just the guy who could really use a friend. So you can tell me – *why did you do it?*"

She looked at him, his face lit only by the moon, and Kat realised she couldn't lie, couldn't con. It felt good somehow to finally say, "Because I could."

When Nick eased away, his hands moved again with a steady, even purpose, flipping through the cards, his fingers like the lightning that flickered in the distance, striking at some foreign shore.

"Your turn," she told him. "I thought you wanted to be one of the good guys."

His fingers stopped; the cards stayed still. "Yeah, well, being an accessory to the art heist of the century has a tendency to change that – even if your mom can keep you from being formally charged with anything."

"So the move to headquarters..." Kat started.

"Not exactly a promotion," he told her. "Now she's stuck there until she can get a big catch and jump-start her career again. And I'm stuck being Disappointing Child of the Year until...well...who knows how long." He tapped the deck, splayed the cards out and back again. "So I came here. I figured that if I'm going to get the blame, I might as well get to have some of the fun."

"It's not fun," Kat told him.

He looked around at the yacht and the stars. "Yeah.

Obviously, this is torture."

"No, Nick. It's dangerous and crazy and people get hurt. I get people hurt."

"You've changed, Kat," Nick told her, and Kat started to protest, but knew, somehow, to save her breath. Nick eased onto one of the lounge chairs, his eyes still staring at the cards. "I knew it the second I saw you in Lyon, running through the basement like—"

"*You saw him in Lyon?*"

Kat wanted to think the lightning had come – that the storm was closer – but it wasn't the rumble of thunder. She knew that even before she turned and saw Hale framed in the light of the door.

"Answer me, Kat. Did you see him in Lyon?"

"Yes. For just a second. It was—"

"Why didn't you tell me?" Hale moved towards her, and she was glad for the dark.

"Everything was happening so fast and...it was just for a second!"

There was an anger in Hale's eyes, but something more than that. A hurt that went deeper than Kat had ever seen. "You should have told me."

Nick laughed. "I don't think she reports to you."

"You really don't get it, new guy." Hale shook his head and stepped away. "She doesn't report to *anyone*."

When Hale turned and started for the opposite side of the deck, Kat was the only one who followed.

"I *kissed* you!"

Kat hadn't meant to yell it, but she wasn't exactly sorry she did. The words had been there, throbbing like a pulse for weeks. She felt lighter without them – one more thing she didn't have to carry.

"In New York – in the limo – I kissed you."

Hale stopped. "I remember."

"I kissed you, and you left. So either I am not someone you want to be kissing..."

"No." He shook his head slowly. "That's not it."

"Or I am a really *bad* kisser." Kat couldn't stop herself from going through the reasons – through the options – like it was just another con and she could master it if only her mind would stop spinning.

"Kat—" He reached for her, but her reflexes were too strong.

She pulled away and looked at him. "I kissed you and you left."

When Kat heard the pounding, she thought it was the beating of her heart. It was too loud, she thought. Hale was going to hear it; he was going to see it; and he was going to know how much power he had to hurt her.

"Hale," she started, but the noise was louder then, echoing from inside. "Hale, I—"

"They're coming." Simon held to the door frame and virtually swung himself out onto the deck. "Kelly!" His breath came in short ragged spurts. "I was listening to LaFont's calls tonight. He talked to New York – to Kelly." He took a deep breath. "And now the Cleopatra...it's coming to the ball!"

ONE DAY UNTIL
THE AUCTION

MONTE CARLO,
MONACO

THIRTY-THREE

There are many things a halfway decent thief must be able to do. The picking of locks is essential. The ability to stay cool in any situation is a must. But sometimes, the most important thing a thief can do...is watch. And wait.

Kat stood by Hale's side, staring down at the two-lane highway that curved like a snake, winding through the cliffs and tunnels into the heart of the city with its ancient buildings and flashy cars. Boutiques, hotels, and of course, a casino.

And more security than even Katarina Bishop had ever seen.

"So the Cleopatra is really coming," she said.

"The Cleopatra is really coming," he agreed.

That the *real* Cleopatra was already there, locked safely away in a vault beneath the most secure bank on the Riviera was a detail that none of them had to mention.

All that really mattered was that Marc Antony was dead and Cleopatra was gone, and the world's elite were on their way to Monaco to spend one night dancing and drinking in the presence of the stones that, if the legends were to be believed, had doomed them both.

In an unprecedented move, the Casino de Monte-Carlo was closed to the public on that day. Kat watched it all through her favourite binoculars as she stood at the top of the ridge. The florists arrived with their flowers. The deliveries of fruit and pastries and meat began promptly at ten. The harbour, always busy in winter, was at full capacity – white dots bobbing on the waves, stretching far out into the deep blue sea. The world's eyes, it seemed, were turned to Monte Carlo. Kat's gaze, however, stayed locked on the casino's doors.

"What changes do they have in store, Simon?"

Marcus had spread a blanket on the grass beneath a tree and served a cold lunch of bread and cheese.

Hale eyed the curvy road. "Maybe I'll come race in the Grand Prix next year... You know I'm an excellent driver."

"By 'you', you mean Marcus, right?" Gabrielle asked.

Hale smirked. "Of course."

"Simon!" Kat yelled this time, and the boy sat upright on the blanket and pulled the headphones off his ears.

"What?" he said, his mouth full of baguette and Brie.

"What have they changed?" Hale asked for her.

"Oh." Simon chewed and swallowed. "Kelly is bringing his own guards for his emerald, so...double what we had down for that."

Kat nodded. "OK."

"And he's asked for thermal-imaging cameras to be trained on the cases."

Hale cut his eyes at Kat, who waved the worry away.

"What about the platform?" she asked.

"You mean the platform with the pressure-sensitive floor sensors that will surround the bulletproof and heavily guarded cases for five feet in any direction?" Hamish asked.

Kat looked at him. "Yes, that floor. Does it still rotate?"

"Yes." Simon shrugged. "I guess that was good enough for Kelly. From what LaFont's been saying all day, there's no change to the floor or the platform itself, just..."

"Doubling everything," Hale finished for him.

"Uh-huh." Simon swallowed hard again, this time for an entirely different reason. "Cases, cameras, guards...this thing just got...bigger."

Kat raised the binoculars to her eyes. When security officers began to roll two massive cases towards the service entrance, Kat knew exactly what she was seeing: four inches of shatterproof, bulletproof, drill-proof glass with a lock made from pure titanium by the best master craftsmen in Switzerland (and everyone knows that when it comes to locks, nobody beats the Swiss).

Kat had known those facts for days, of course, but seeing and knowing can be two very different things, so that's why she stared down at the scene below as if the reality might be in some way different, as if the picture in 3-D and moving colour might show some hole, some contrast, some gap that might go unnoticed on blueprints made of paper in black-and-white.

"Kelly is bringing the emerald personally?" Kat asked, with

a worried look at Hale.

"Oh yeah," Simon answered. "And LaFont doesn't sound too happy about that."

"I bet he doesn't," Gabrielle said. "I hate that Kelly guy. I'd love to see him get his."

"One job at a time, Gabs," Hale told her. "One job at a time." When they turned to walk away, Hale reached out for Kat and caught her arm. "You sure about this?" he asked.

"If it works, it works," Kat told him.

"And if it doesn't?" he asked.

She looked at him. "If it doesn't, then I've heard Monaco has the nicest prisons in all of Europe."

"It does," both Hamish and Angus said in unison.

And with that, it was decided.

THIRTY-FOUR

For having such an impractical profession, Pierre LaFont had always been a very practical man. Protocols were meant to be followed, he always said. Rules were meant to be adhered to, and guidelines were *not* suggestions. So that was why the guards at the doors had such strict orders that no one was to enter without an invitation. It was why he was so incredibly annoyed when the young woman in charge of entertainment told him that the spotlights would be at sixty-degree angles instead of seventy, that the violinist had called in sick and her role would be filled by a viola player instead.

As he examined the casino floor twenty minutes before the ball was to begin, everything *looked* perfect. But the devil was in the details, LaFont had always said. And on that night – that night, the devil...was Maggie.

"The ropes should be at least two feet further from the platform," she said, surveying the scene.

"I want that flag taken down," she'd told one guard, for no apparent reason. "Yes, that flag! The one there by that camera."

But her most unusual demand was reserved for Monsieur LaFont himself. "Promise me, Pierre," she'd told him. "Promise me, *no kids*."

"I can assure you, madam, that this is not an event for children."

"I mean it, Pierre. You or your people see a kid – any kid – they also see the door." Her voice stayed loud and brash, but there was something else about her right then, and it occurred to him that her big Texas bravado might be a bit of a fake. But fakes are part of the territory, LaFont told himself. All he needed to remember was that the Antony – and its commission – were very, very real.

So he moved the flag and reset the ropes and took his place at the top of the stairs, looking down at the party of the century, certain Maggie was right about one thing: this was not the place for children.

Of all the parties that had taken place in Monte Carlo in the last century, that particular ball was destined from the beginning to become a thing of legend. Never before had the casino been closed for such an event. Even for Monaco, the guest list was elite and grand and famous.

But the most impressive thing about that very impressive building was actually in the centre of the floor. A small platform sat, rotating. There were glass cases on pedestals, and as the platform spun, the cases caught the light, sending it spinning slowly around the room.

Red velvet ropes surrounded it, keeping the people at

bay, and yet they flocked towards the little stage and the empty cases. For two thousand years, people had looked for the Antony Emerald. And on that night, the world's elite were willing to pay a small fortune just to see the air where it might sit.

Well, almost all of the elite.

"I'm sorry, young lady, but your name is not on the list."

"He knows me!" Kat yelled, and pointed through the crowd, towards LaFont, who had tried (and failed) to turn away in time. "Pierre!" she yelled. "Oh, Monsieur LaFont!"

"What is the problem here?" LaFont looked and sounded like a man who had far more important things to do, and the young attendant knew it.

"She has no credentials," the attendant snapped, as if it were all Kat's fault.

"Pierre," Kat pleaded. "It's *me*!" Her whisper echoed through the crowd.

"Yes, yes," Pierre hissed, quieting her.

"Pierre, I need to see my aunt Maggie." Kat grasped the shopping bag in her hands. "She sent me out to get her stuff, and she needs it."

"Yes, I hear you," the man said. "But your aunt has very strict guidelines about who shall be admitted this evening."

"Oh, Pierre!" Kat laughed and slapped his arm. "You're a hoot. Anyone ever tell you that?"

"No, miss. You are, quite honestly, the first."

His gaze swept around the entry hall.

"Pierre!" Kat hissed again. She tried to wriggle free, but

the guards blocked her path again. "Have you ever seen Maggie without her eyeliner? No, you haven't." She waved a small cosmetics case in his direction. "And I'm here to make sure you never will."

"Sir," the guard said, struggling to hold on to Kat's wriggling arm. "Sir, I—"

"Let her in," Pierre said, jerking his head towards the very short, very annoying American. "Go," he snapped at Kat.

When LaFont turned back to the party, it truly seemed to be the perfect night. Well...he forced a smile, raised his hand and shouted through the crowd, "Mr Kelly, so good to see you."

Almost perfect.

When Oliver Kelly the Third took his rival's hand, it was almost as an afterthought. He looked over the room, the food, and finally, the empty cases. "I supposed everything is in order?"

"Oh, certainly. The only thing we need is for you to add your stone to the auction block tomorrow." LaFont gave a nervous laugh.

"No," Kelly said coolly. "That will not be happening."

"Of course," LaFont said with a smile. "We're so happy that you and the Cleopatra could join us for the evening. I know Madame Maggie was most enthusiastic about the prospect of seeing the stones united at last."

Kelly eyed him as if he were an inferior businessman who had got lucky. Once. "Indeed."

"Excuse me, Monsieur LaFont," a deep voice said, and only then did he notice that Oliver Kelly had not come to the party alone. "We meet again," said the young man he'd met in the hotel lobby – the one who had complimented his car. "My name is Colin Knightsbury." He gestured to the gorgeous young woman beside him. "This is Ms Melanie McDonald. We insure the Cleopatra."

"*Bonjour*," LaFont said, reaching for Hale's hand. "We are so pleased that you and the mademoiselle can—"

"Sorry, LaFont," Oliver Kelly said, cutting in. "I'll see you later."

He was already turning, walking away, when the young woman called, "Wait!" She draped her arm through Oliver Kelly's. "If you don't mind, I'll walk with you."

Kelly smiled. "I don't mind at all."

Kat saw it all from her place in the centre of the casino floor – the way Gabrielle stayed close to Kelly's side, the ease with which Hale spoke to LaFont. So far, so good, she had to think. She reminded herself it was a simple plan – basic and plain, but not foolproof. Nothing, after all, was ever guaranteed.

And yet, walking through the crowds, Kat expected to feel the rush her cousin had spoken of – the high – but she didn't, and that in itself was a source of some concern. She looked at her fingers, but they didn't shake. She placed a hand on her stomach, but there was no telltale flutter of nerves. All in all, she felt...normal. Across the room she saw Hale break away from LaFont and make a beeline in her direction.

"What's wrong with you?" Hale asked. Kat's arms seemed especially small in his strong grasp as he pulled her to a dark and quiet corner of the room.

"I'm fine."

"Yeah." He stepped closer. "That's my point. This is serious, Kat."

"I know."

"This goes off the tracks and we might not get it back."

She looked at him. "What's your point, Hale?"

"So you got conned... So you're human..." He ran a hand through his hair and took a step back. "So you're mortal like the rest of us." He looked away, then back again. "Is that so bad?"

"What are you saying?"

"I'm saying what I said in New York. We could go anywhere. We could do anything." He brushed a stray piece of hair behind her ear. "We don't have to do *this*."

It wasn't often that Kat wished she could go back in time. The world didn't work that way, after all. There was no such thing as a second chance. But even as Hale said the words, she knew they were true – they could board a jet and disappear, haul up anchor and be in Casablanca before anyone even knew that they were missing. She could never change the mistake she'd made before, but nothing said she had to make the same mistake again. And for a second, she felt herself teetering, fighting the urge to run.

Run.

To boarding school and Moscow and Rio.

Run.

To a snowy cabin at the top of the world.

And right then, Kat knew it hadn't begun with a lie in a diner in the rain – that the chase hadn't lasted weeks – but decades. And the job that had started in Montreal had to end in Monte Carlo.

"Hale," Kat said, but before she could finish, Simon's voice was in her ear, saying, "Kat, Maggie is moving into position. Kat, did you copy?"

"Don't worry." She looked at Hale. "I hear you."

And then the lights went out.

THIRTY-FIVE

To say that Katarina Bishop was at home in the dark wouldn't be entirely correct. She did not have sonar like a bat. Her eyes did not process light and shadow differently, like a cat's. But if Hale was at home in his six-thousand-dollar tuxedo amid the trays of champagne and caviar, then Kat herself was perfectly at ease standing in the shadows of the ballroom, surrounded by jewels and wallets and other people's money.

Still, when the spotlights flickered on, bright beams slicing through the ballroom and onto the cases that stood empty and waiting on the small platform, Kat was like everybody else who stood waiting, needing to know what was about to happen.

"Kat?" Simon whispered, the word echoing through her ear.

"It's time."

No one saw her say it. All of Monaco was too busy staring at those two cases and the man who stood between them, a microphone in his hand, looking out over the crowd, mentally counting his money.

"*Messieurs et mesdames*, ladies and gentlemen," Pierre LaFont addressed the crowd, "thank you so much for coming to celebrate with us tonight the greatest cultural find of the twenty-first century." Polite applause filled the room. Only a single whoop echoed out, and Kat made a mental note to have a word with Hamish once this was all over.

"I am very grateful to Monsieur Oliver Kelly for generously allowing us to share with you..." He paused for dramatic effect, and then swept his arms towards the case on his right and cried, "The Cleopatra Emerald!"

There was no applause, only a faint but steady clicking sound so slight it would have disappeared entirely in any other moment, in any other room. The platform had stopped spinning, and yet the case itself seemed to move, hydraulics working, smoothly raising the green stone from the casino's vaults below. There was a gasp in the crowd when it came to the surface, but the silence returned almost immediately in its wake.

And the crowd stood – waiting.

People are all the same, as every decent con man knows. They have the same needs. The same wants. Every person in that room wanted to touch history. To feel fame. To hold love – hold it in the palms of two hands.

And that was why they stood in silence, watching, waiting for Pierre LaFont to say, "And now, ladies and gentlemen, I give to you for the first time in two thousand years, the Antony Emerald."

Again there was the whirling sound, the sight of something

rising inside a protective case. But no one seemed to believe what they were seeing until the lights caught the second stone and the platform began to spin, sending the Cleopatra and the Antony on a turn around the ballroom.

Only the small signs that hung on the two cases gave any clue that what the crowd was seeing wasn't a mirror image, some elaborate mirage. The stones were identical. Perfect. Priceless and pristine.

They're here. They're real. And they're together, the whole room seemed to think.

But not Kat. Kat stood silently in the centre of the crowd, thinking, Charlie is a genius.

As the emeralds turned, they seemed to catch the light, covering the casino in a kaleidoscope of green, and yet it was nothing compared to the look in Hale's eyes as he stood across the crowded room, staring right at Kat.

She felt like just another girl at the ball in that moment, just another person needing it to be real – a romance that had spanned two thousand years. A love that had overcome geography and class and time.

She wanted to believe in that. She looked at Hale and knew he wanted it too.

On the stage, LaFont was still speaking; the crowd was still staring. It was a moment that had been a millennium in the making, but it was also a moment built on a lie, and as badly as Kat wanted to believe it, she knew better than to trust the con.

"Simon?" Kat asked.

"We're good," he said through the small comms unit in her ear.

"Hamish, what about you and Angus?"

"We're in position, love," was Angus's reply.

"Gabrielle," Kat said, "what about Kelly?"

"Covered," her cousin whispered.

And then there were two, Kat thought. She felt Nick moving towards her, heard him say, "Kat, are you sure you want to do this?" But through the crowd, all she could see was Hale.

"Now," she said while, ten feet away, the emerald stood gleaming in its case. It was somehow smaller than Kat remembered. "We end this. Now."

THIRTY-SIX

The band still played. The food still flowed. But the room had taken on a different feel as Nick walked away from Kat and through the crowd. No one even noticed the young man with the too-big tuxedo who pushed against the current of people who were moving towards the glistening green stones in the spotlight.

"Leave her alone." Hale's voice was rough and deep and didn't at all match the cover he was wearing.

"I think she knows what she wants," Nick hissed, trying to avoid a scene.

"It's time you left her alone," Hale said again, closing the distance between them, forcing Nick out into the hallway, away from the crowd and the jewels and the world on the other side of the door.

"If you don't like me, all you have to do is say so," Nick said.

"No, I don't think I have to *say* anything."

There were footsteps in the hall behind them, but neither boy turned to look.

"She's a big girl," Nick said.

"She's five-two."

"I wasn't speaking—"

"Maybe you don't understand." Hale stepped even closer. "Stay away from—"

But Hale never finished, because his fist was suddenly flying through the air. It struck Nick on the jaw, and sent the smaller boy spinning, the sound echoing in the empty hallway.

No. Wait, the two of them seemed to realise.

Almost empty hallway.

In the next instant, Pierre LaFont was upon them, two guards at his side. "Stop this!" LaFont yelled. "Stop... Mr Knightsbury?" LaFont's eyes went wide as he pulled Hale off Nick.

"Ha!" Nick laughed, but the sound was pure hatred. He struggled to his feet, clawing at LaFont to get closer to Hale.

"Stay out of this!" Hale shouted at LaFont.

"Quiet, you two," LaFont said, looking from the two of them to the social event of the year that was under way just through the open doors. "In here!" LaFont motioned at the guards, who grabbed Nick and Hale and pulled them into a small room normally reserved for high-stakes card games and VIP parties.

Hale walked to the far side of the room, while Nick paced by the door.

"You!" LaFont wiped his brow. "I'm shocked at you,

Mr Knightsbury. Where is Monsieur Kelly?" he asked one of the guards. "Find him. Bring him here."

"Oh," Hale said slowly. "I think he's probably busy."

"Well," LaFont huffed, "make no mistake, I will be reporting this to your superiors."

Hale flexed his hand as if it still hurt. But Nick just laughed. "Yeah. You go ahead and do that."

Hale jerked again, but the guards lunged forward, keeping him away from Nick.

"LaFont!" The woman's voice rang out just as the doors flew open and Hale skidded to a halt. Maggie's eyes were wild, and her gaze was locked on the man at the front of the room. "Where have you..."

And then she stopped. She turned slowly, looking from Nick's swelling lips to the guards, and finally her gaze came to rest on Hale, who stood struggling against their grasp.

A knowing look filled her eyes when she said, "Well, well. What do we have here?"

LaFont rushed forward. "Oh, madame, please return to the party. As you can see, our security has this little skirmish well in hand."

"I'll be the judge of that, Pierre."

"Of course, but as you can see, Monsieur Knightsbury has had an altercation with this young man regarding..." LaFont trailed off. "Why were you fighting?" he asked.

"Oh." Nick wiped his mouth. Blood stained the white sleeve. "Just some girl."

"You." Maggie pointed at one of the guards. "Take them

both outside. Now."

Maggie's face stayed frozen, her posture perfectly even as the young man dived in front of her, almost knocking her off her feet as he clawed at Hale. Guards lunged for him in return, but when they finally separated the two, the whole room stood still and silent.

"Now!" Maggie hissed.

"Find Mr Kelly," LaFont told one of the guards who had appeared in Maggie's wake. He gestured to another guard and then to Nick. "And see these young men outside."

When the guard reached for Nick, he jerked away.

"You really can have her," Nick said, wiping his sleeve across his mouth again. He stared down at the blood and closed the door behind him.

In the silence that came next, no one seemed to know what to do.

LaFont walked to Maggie, placed a hand on her shoulder as if she were someone who needed comfort and protection in times of great distress. But there was an entirely different sort of look in Maggie's eyes as she glared at Hale. Part fear, part worry, part outrage and disbelief.

"Get this one too, Pierre. I've been in enough bar brawls in my life to know one's a quick way to ruin a party."

She picked up her skirts and turned, but not before Hale could call, "It's good to see you too...*Margaret*."

Hale leaned against a poker table and studied LaFont, who shouted, "What are you talking about?" He sounded like a man on the verge of a very hard fall. "Monsieur Knightsbury, what do you have to say for yourself?"

Maggie stopped and turned. The bravado was gone, replaced by icy steel when Maggie said, "Pierre, show him the door. *Now.*"

THIRTY-SEVEN

Luck is a strange thing in the life of any thief and halfway decent con man. What is it that keeps the mark from counting the till or the guards from looking up at precisely the wrong moment? Kat had learned at a very young age that luck is for the amateur, the lazy – those who are unprepared and unskilled. And yet she also knew that luck, like most things, cannot be truly missed until it is also truly gone.

Or so it certainly seemed as Kat watched Nick walk towards her, a guard two steps behind. His clothes were a mess and his face was bleeding. Cursed didn't even begin to describe his appearance when he leaned close to Kat's ear, held her hand in his for one brief second, and whispered, "We're done."

And then Kat was alone in the centre of the ballroom, watching Nick disappear. When she turned, she saw Hale at LaFont's side, bloody and shamed. The Bagshaws had disappeared in the crowd like smoke. Simon's voice was all that remained.

"What's happening?" she heard him say. "There's chatter

on the security channels saying they're looking for someone. They're looking for—"

"Monsieur Kelly!" one of the guards called. Kat saw them point towards the Cleopatra's owner and the elegant young woman standing at his side. "Monsieur Kelly!" the man called again.

Kat watched Gabrielle twirl, spinning on the stairs, and – in a flash – it happened. Her high heel seemed to catch in the hem of her long gown, and she faltered, tumbling towards the railing, while Oliver Kelly the Third, stood helpless, watching the most beautiful girl in the room fall over the edge.

Gabrielle yelled, and the crowd gasped, watching her grab for one of the spotlights that was trained on the cases below. The light swirled around the room as she tried to steady herself, but it was too late, and gravity was too strong, and the spotlight broke free beneath her grasp.

The cry that followed was deeper and sharper than the one that had filled the room only seconds before. The girl dropped at least a foot and then reached for a cable that ran between the lights. It was too loose, someone later noted. A workman must have been slacking on the job, but it seemed like the most fortunate mistake in the world as the girl clung to it. But just then the cable snapped at one end, and suddenly the girl was swinging across the floor, like Tarzan's Jane clinging to a vine.

Her gown was long and pink, and it swayed like a ribbon as she yelled and clung to the cable for dear life.

"Help her!" Oliver Kelly screamed.

The people nearest the rail were in the best position to see the Bagshaws rush towards her. One tried reaching for her, knocking the green bunting free of the rail, sending it trailing over the bank of surveillance cameras below, but it was too late.

"Ah!" she screamed again. The cable jerked, unsteady under her weight. The lights flickered. Once. Twice. Sparks flew, and then the entire ballroom was shrouded in black.

"You there!" someone called to the pair of guards stationed by the stones. "Help us!" the man yelled as, up above, the young woman's hands slipped and she kicked as if trying to gain her footing in mid-air. One of her high heels slipped from her delicate foot. It tumbled end over end and then landed on the pressure-sensitive rotating platform behind the velvet ropes, causing the sirens to scream, piercing the air.

The girl's grip slackened once again, and it seemed as if the entire room was holding its breath. Or maybe, Kat thought, it was just her when she heard Simon's voice say, "Kat, the cameras are blocked. You're clear. You're clear *now*."

At some point along the way, Kat must have lost the feeling in her fingers. She unclenched her hands and looked down at the key that Nick had passed her in that split second before the chaos began. The impression was still on her palm, and she knew it was now or never.

She didn't dare look up. She didn't run, and she didn't walk. She just moved as only a thief can move. It was as if the wind had blown her to the other side of the ropes, and she stood shrouded in the darkness, listening to the sirens and the shouts of two hundred people who stood watching, waiting for a girl to fall.

Kat willed her hand not to tremble. She called upon every ounce of cool in her veins as she knelt beside the case and gripped the key.

"She's slipping! Catch her!" someone yelled.

But Kat didn't dare glance away from the cases. She looked from the Antony to the Cleopatra and back again, studying the signs that were, to the naked eye, the only indication that the stones were not simply mirror images of each other. Then, with the key in her hand and the platform still spinning, Kat took a deep breath and reached for them.

"I don't think so!" a voice cried a moment later, and Kat felt someone catch her wrist, jerk her from the platform and onto the hardwood floor.

Her knees ached, and her head spun with the sound of the pulsing sirens; but nothing compared to the rage she felt when Maggie leaned down and whispered, "I invented the Cinderella, little girl."

Maggie sounded like a young woman. She seemed impossibly strong as she pulled Kat to her feet and wrenched the key from her hand. She appeared almost insulted when she snapped, "Did you honestly think this would work? Did you honestly think you could take my emerald and carry it out the front door?"

It was an excellent question, Kat couldn't help but think,

as she stood, almost trembling, staring at the figure in the shadows behind Maggie. She studied the posture, felt the presence; and even before the deep voice said, "Hello, Katarina," she knew Charlie, the forger – her uncle Charlie, the exit strategy – was a long, long way from Monte Carlo.

"Hello, Uncle Eddie." There was no panic in her voice. The sadness, unfortunately, was a far harder thing to hide. "What brings you to town?"

Her uncle stepped closer, and she watched him smile, his eyes filled with shame and disappointment, and Kat knew she hadn't just been caught. She'd been conned. Again.

"My brother, Charles, was kind enough to tell me that you came to see him. He's sorry he could not come to Monaco himself, but he doesn't get out as much as he once did. It seemed only fitting that I should...*fill in*."

Kat wasn't sure what she should feel in that moment. Shock or anger, exhaustion or betrayal? So instead she just looked at Uncle Eddie.

"It was you. There was a moment on the boat when I thought..." She trailed off, realising that the curse had finally caught up with her, but it was just as well. She was far too tired of running. Her voice was soft, defeated, as she whispered, "It was always you."

In hindsight, Kat realised, she should have felt a degree of panic, maybe a surge of anger or shame. And perhaps she would have if the emergency floodlights hadn't flickered to life.

"The emeralds!" someone yelled, and Kat felt the room's

attention shift. She knew what it must look like – the sight of a shorter-than-average girl and the infamous Maggie standing so close to the cases, sirens sounding all around them.

A catastrophe was one thing, the hushed room seemed to say. A scandal quite another.

"Madame Maggie!" LaFont yelled, running through the room, right past where Hamish and Angus were helping a very pale Gabrielle down a ladder.

"Madame, are you all right?" LaFont looked from Maggie then to the Antony. "What is the meaning of this?" he snapped at Kat. "No one is supposed to be so close to the emeralds!" He yelled something in French to the guards, who reclaimed their positions.

"Mademoiselle, what do you have to say for yourself?" LaFont hissed at Kat, the words carrying through the crowd of people, all of whom seemed to be wondering the same thing.

"Yes, Aunt Maggie..." Kat looked up at the older woman. Her smile was a challenge, a dare. "What *do* I have to say?"

Kat could feel the crowd staring, their collective hearts pounding. Someone turned the sirens off, and a single spotlight came to life. Kat stood in its glare, feeling something that no thief is ever supposed to feel.

But fortunately, she wasn't standing there alone.

"My niece was..." Maggie started slowly. "She was..."

Kat picked up the satin pump that lay on the platform, held it close to her chest, and told LaFont, "That girl is going to be needing her shoe."

THIRTY-EIGHT

It did not happen often that Katarina Bishop felt small. Petite she could not deny. Short was a scientific fact. But there were no mirrors in Uncle Eddie's kitchen, no gauge, no scale, no way to see all the ways that she, the shortest, lightest, youngest member of the family, had never really fit the physical mould.

But standing beside Maggie in the private elevator twenty minutes later, zooming to the presidential suite, Kat felt tiny, minuscule. As insignificant as dust.

When the doors slid open and she heard Uncle Eddie say, "Welcome back, Katarina," it felt like the wind, blowing what was left of her away.

Kat didn't want to step inside, but she had to. She would have traded anything – stolen anything – to have found a way out, but they were forty storeys high and the elevator was closing, and even curseless, Kat knew that was a long, long way to climb.

"What?" Kat looked around. "No tower to lock me up in?"

Maggie laughed. "I think this will do."

Two large men in dark suits flanked the elevator doors.

Another stood on the opposite side of the room. But there was only one man in the suite who really mattered.

There, in the well-lit room, Kat looked at him closely. "I wasn't expecting to see *you* for a while," she told him.

He smiled in a way that was completely different from his brother. There was nothing of Charlie in his eyes when he said, "I know."

"You know what she did, don't you?" Kat asked.

Eddie didn't answer, but the quick glance he gave Maggie spoke volumes.

Kat gave a joyless laugh. "I mean, here I thought that the Chelovek Pseudonimas were only supposed to be used in special circumstances – I thought they were *sacred*. She used a Pseudonima for fun and profit, Uncle Eddie," Kat shouted. "But maybe you don't care about that... Maybe there are exceptions for old girlfriends."

"Katarina." The word was a hiss – a warning.

Maggie turned to the guards and commanded, "Outside." Together, the goons made their way towards the doors. "But don't go far," Maggie added, as if Kat were dangerous. And in that moment, Kat had to laugh. Because in that moment, she was.

"She used the name Romani. Did you know that?" Kat would have given anything for her voice not to crack, her eyes not to water. But it was too late. There was no turning back the con.

She looked into her uncle's eyes, watched him watching Maggie. And Kat saw it all in that look. Hurt. Pride. Love.

Once upon a time, Uncle Eddie had been in love. Once upon a time, Uncle Eddie had been human. Of all the jobs he'd done and things he'd stolen, Maggie was the one that got away.

"Of course you knew," Kat whispered. She couldn't look at her uncle when she finished, "You know everything."

She reached for the button, started to summon the lift and simply walk away, but Maggie moved to block her path. "I don't think so."

"Oh, gee, thanks for the hospitality, Mags, but I have places to be." Kat looked at Uncle Eddie. "People to check on."

"Your crew is fine," Maggie said. "Pierre never even missed his keys. Foolish man. So do not fear, my dear, you will be perfectly safe here tonight."

Kat laughed. "I'm not staying." She looked at the windows, the locked doors, and found her small hands balling into fists. "Move."

But Maggie simply laughed. It was a terrible, taunting, *Isn't she adorable* sound.

"You're right about her," Maggie said with a glance at Uncle Eddie. "She is a strong one." And then her gaze was back on Kat. "But I can't allow you to leave." She walked to the window, pulled back the curtains, and stared at the lights of the palace that shone on the distant hill.

"Tomorrow morning my emerald will be publicly authenticated and then sold to the highest bidder." Maggie turned slowly. "Until then, Kat, my dear, please consider yourself my *guest*."

Maybe they thought it was more appropriate – or kind – that Uncle Eddie was the one who walked her to the tiny bedroom and locked the door. Kat didn't mention Charlie. She didn't talk about betrayal. Neither of them said they were sorry. It was just the kind of thing that wouldn't do any good to say, so instead, Eddie stopped in the doorway and looked at her.

"So you're finished?" There was a knowing look in Uncle Eddie's eye, a finality to the words, but also a question. A challenge. A dare.

Kat felt the blood rush to her pale cheeks as she said, "It's done."

THE DAY OF
THE AUCTION

MONTE CARLO,
MONACO

THIRTY-NINE

As the sun rose over the small city-state of Monaco that Friday morning, it seemed to bring the gaze of the whole world with it. The streets and beaches were strewn with news trucks and foreign correspondents, reporters looking for a story. The headlines spoke of the ballroom and emeralds, of curses being broken and a beautiful young woman holding on to a cable for dear life.

But for all the stories being beamed around the world on that clear morning, not one mentioned a helicopter hovering near the windows of the presidential suite at Monaco's ritziest hotel. There was no talk of teens rappelling down the side of the building. No holes had been blasted through its side or rescue missions mounted involving stolen maid uniforms, room service carts, and acetylene torches.

No, no one had tried to steal Kat Bishop. And when the sun came up, there was nothing more than a room service tray and clean change of clothes to show that anyone had remembered she was there at all.

It was just as well, Kat realised; she'd never considered

herself the kind of girl who wanted to be rescued.

Or so she thought until the door to her small room opened and Maggie said, "Let's go."

For all the hours that Kat had spent trying to find a way inside the Prince's Palace, there was one she'd never considered: be a hostage. She made a mental note not to rule that out in the future as she sat beside Maggie in the backseat of a Bentley, waiting for the guards to wave them through the gates that, three days before, the Bagshaws had been debating about the best way to blow up.

It had never occurred to her what else she might have to destroy to find a way inside.

"Where's Uncle Eddie?"

"His work here is finished, Katarina. He has other obligations."

Kat nodded and turned back to the window. "Paraguay," she said with a sigh.

"I thought it was Uruguay," Maggie said, then nodded as if it didn't matter, because, in fact, it didn't. "Before he left, your uncle gave me his word that this matter is over."

"It is." There was no lie in Kat's voice when she said it. No angle. No con. "So how's it feel to be so close to pulling it off? You've been chasing this for almost fifty years, Maggie. You've broken a lot of codes to get this far." Kat looked at her squarely. "And hearts."

"Oh, to be so young. So naive. If you haven't noticed, darling, your uncle himself chose to help me. It was his idea to bring the Cleopatra, in fact – double the security, the notoriety. The risk."

"Yeah. That was smart," Kat agreed. "I think that's exactly what I would have done."

Maggie smiled. "Of course you would have, Katarina. You're very good."

"I am good," Kat let herself agree. "But I'm not heartless."

"Of course you are. Or you will be. Don't worry about Charles and Edward, my dear. Your uncles and I know the truth –" she pulled on her gloves and stared through the window – "that love is the biggest con of all."

Kat studied her across the backseat, sun streaming through the windows. Her skin was effervescent, glowing.

"*I'm not you.*"

Had Kat thought the words or had she said them? She wasn't really sure, and didn't really care. She would have been just as happy to shout it from the rooftops. "I won't ever be like you."

"Oh, really?" Maggie said.

"Yeah," Kat said slowly, then turned to look out at the people who surrounded the walls. Some tourists. Some protestors carrying signs about artefacts and raiders and returning to Egypt the emeralds it had borne.

"I will never be heartless or greedy or... I'm not you," Kat said again, the realisation shining on her like the sun.

"Oh." Maggie almost laughed. "And how are we so different?"

A thousand reasons flooded Kat's mind, but there was

only one that really mattered.

"Because I'm not in this alone."

When the car eased forward, the crowd seemed to part, and Kat's eyes found their focus on a single boy in a perfectly tailored suit, a long dark overcoat, and a felt hat she'd once seen in Uncle Eddie's closet.

The gates swung smoothly open, royal guards waving them through, so Kat climbed onto her knees and watched Hale disappear through the back glass. She saw him smile, watched him tip his hat.

But the wink...it was the wink that said, *We're on.*

FORTY

Katarina Bishop was not the first thief to ever see behind the walls at the Prince's Palace. She looked at Maggie and reminded herself that she wasn't the only thief behind them then.

The sounds of their footsteps echoed on the marble floor in the empty corridor. Maggie's high heels sounded like gunfire, and Kat knew Maggie was done hiding, was finished lurking in dark shadows. This was the big job, the last job. Her face would be too well known for a long time after this. The story too infamous. If all went according to plan, Maggie would be leaving the Riviera in a few hours with a cashier's cheque and the title of Greatest Living Con.

But she would never be Visily Romani.

So Kat focused on the footsteps. She could feel herself counting from the door.

Twenty-seven paces. Air shaft.

Thirteen steps, double doors.

Pass another corridor.

Ten steps.

Through another door.

Windows to the cliffs.

Five steps.

The blueprints were taking shape in her mind. She remembered everything until she heard the whirling sound of the elevator and Maggie snapping, "Katarina!" The woman grabbed her arm and pulled her through an open door. "Come," was the order.

Kat had spent days wondering where the nerve centre of palace security must be, and when she finally stepped into the room, she found it. Monitors covered three walls. There were live shots from all over the buildings and grounds. One screen flashed with crowd scenes, and Kat found herself looking for Hale's dark coat and the telltale hat, but he was gone without a trace to show he'd been there at all.

"Madame Maggie, welcome," LaFont said, rushing forward. "It is a fine day indeed, and—"

"Is this all of it?" Maggie snapped, looking around the room as if she had expected more.

Kat laughed; Maggie glared.

"That's a Remington 760 security nerve centre with the artificial intelligence chip and backup encryption. It's what they use at Buckingham Palace," Kat explained, then remembered where she was and who she was supposed to be, so she giggled. "Or so I heard."

"This has facial recognition software?" Maggie asked.

"Of course!" Kat and the security head said at the same time, both sounding more than a little indignant.

Maggie slipped an arm around Kat's shoulders and gripped tightly. Kat mouthed the words *I bruise*, but the pressure didn't subside until Maggie handed the security head a small drive and he inserted it into the machine. Six familiar faces began to flash across the screen.

"They're...kids," the security head said, but Maggie seemed immune to that particular objection.

"Distribute hard copies to your men," she ordered. "If you see any of these people, bring them immediately to me."

The security head looked at Pierre LaFont as if he must be missing something, and he was. Kat knew it as soon as the monitors flickered. She thought of the whirling sound of the lift, the size and scope of the ventilation shafts. And finally, the look on Hale's face and the wink.

"Madame," LaFont said. "Madame, Monsieur Kelly is here."

"Thank you, gentlemen," Maggie told the officers who filled the room. She turned back to the door and the auction and her future. She gripped Kat's arm a little tighter. "Thank you very much indeed."

There is a sensation that comes in the midst of any job. Walking down the halls between Maggie and LaFont, Kat felt it – a pulse, a charge. Goose bumps covered her arms as if a storm were blowing in, like she'd dragged her feet, touched a doorknob, felt a spark.

"What is it?" Maggie asked, spinning on her. "Why are you smiling?"

"You don't feel it?" Kat asked. She kept her pace beside Maggie. "You will."

"What do you mean?"

"You'll see."

But Maggie did not seem worried – not with Kat beside her and the guards at their backs.

Soon she was yelling, "Mr Kelly!" her big booming voice breaking through the reverent silence of the hall.

Kat had seen the crowded foyer on the monitors, but the palace was large and like a maze, and she knew they were far away from the auction and the emerald – no one from Kat's crew was going to hear the scream.

"We have ten minutes, Madame," LaFont said.

"Thank you, Pierre." Maggie's gaze was steely as she stood staring at the pristine man from New York. "So tell me, Mr Kelly, what can I do for you?"

"I'm sorry, ma'am, I was under the impression that it was you who had asked to see me."

"Not me, darlin'," Maggie said, patting his arm. Despite everything, Kat had to admire the woman before her. The accent was spot-on, the word choice simply perfect.

Kelly, on the other hand, looked significantly less impressed. "I was told to meet you here ten minutes before the start of the auction."

"I don't know what to say, sweetie," Maggie told him. "You must have me mistaken for some other about-to-be-filthier-rich woman." She gave a throaty laugh, but Kelly didn't join in.

"Very well," he said. "I suppose I will wish you luck."

He was turning to leave when LaFont called, "Madame, His Royal Highness has asked for a moment of your time."

Maggie started after LaFont, but then stopped suddenly and turned back to Kelly.

"You say someone told you to meet me here?" she asked the man who was reaching for the lift call button.

"Yes," Kelly said.

Maggie seemed to consider this just as the doors were sliding open. "Who?" she asked.

"That insurance man. I believe Knightsbury is his name."

It only took a second for Maggie to recognise it – for the pieces to fall into place. But Kat had been right, it seemed. The Long Con never was truly long – just a few million moments strung together, and *that* moment was just long enough for Kat to jump into the lift beside Oliver Kelly.

Long enough for her to call, "I'll meet you at the auction, Aunt Maggie!"

Long enough for Maggie to curse and watch Kat disappear behind the sliding doors.

Oliver Kelly was not in the business of antiques. He didn't pay his bills with old family paintings and Grandmother's pearls. True, that was how it seemed to the world, but Kelly himself knew better. He was in the business of details. A name remembered. A card sent. A forgery noticed and weeded out before it could tarnish anything else that it might touch.

Still, standing in the small lift, floating through the walls of the Prince's Palace, it was easy to ignore the young girl who stood beside him. She was no doubt too poor to buy and she seemed too worthless to sell, so he kept his eyes on his own reflection in the mirrored doors.

When the lift hesitated and rattled, Kelly punched frantically at the buttons. When the lift froze, he pushed the buttons harder. Only the soft voice saying, "It won't do any good," reminded him – the king of details – that he was not in that small space alone.

There was a slight rattling overhead, and Kelly's gaze flew upwards. "It sounds like someone's up there," he said.

The girl laughed. "Maybe a ghost." But Oliver Kelly saw nothing at all funny about the situation.

"What's wrong?" the girl asked. "Don't you believe in ghosts, Mr Kelly?"

"That's absurd." He banged at the doors, "Hello! Hello, out there!"

But the girl didn't seem the least bit panicked as she inched closer in the small space. "What about curses – do you believe in them?"

He punched the buttons again – all of them. The girl must have thought that was hilarious, because she laughed and leaned against the wall. There was a slight tilt to her head when she told him, "I thought you'd be more like your grandfather. He didn't scare easily, did he?"

Only then did Kelly whirl on the girl beside him. "My grandfather was a brave man – a visionary."

"A thief?"

She said it so easily, with such little shame or disdain that he could have sworn he'd misheard her. She looked innocent enough, after all, leaning there with her hands resting against the rail at the small of her back.

"Pardon me?" Kelly asked.

"I don't think I could do it – rob a tomb in the middle of the desert... I mean, I know he didn't go alone, but he would have kept the crew small. And it would have been hard...for an amateur...cleaning out the entire chamber in just a couple of days."

"Young lady, you have no idea of what you speak."

But the girl just laughed. She looked and sounded far older than she should have when she smiled and said, "Actually, I do."

The man turned back to the controls. "There should be a..." He let his voice trail off, still searching among the buttons and lights.

"They didn't start putting telephones in lifts until 1972," she told him flatly. "This is an Otis 420." He stared at her. "Manufactured primarily in Europe in the 1940s." She shook her head. "No phones."

It was then that Oliver Kelly felt himself begin to panic.

"Breathe, Mr Kelly. It's OK. I'm sure we're fine. After all, it's not like one of us is cursed."

"The Cleopatra Emerald is not cursed!"

But the girl just smiled, as if she knew better. The look in her blue eyes said that she knew everything.

"He took it, didn't he?" the girl asked while Kelly pulled at his tie. "What I can't decide is if he joined the Millers' expedition for the purpose of double-crossing them or if it was just dumb luck."

"My grandfather was not dumb," Kelly snarled.

"Of course he wasn't." The girl sounded so forthright, so sincere, it was almost easy to forget what she was saying. "If you ask me," she added, "he was a genius." The lift rumbled but didn't move. "That much treasure? It might have been the heist of the century."

"Oliver Kelly was no common criminal!"

The girl smiled. "Who said anything about common?" She moved closer, taking more than half the space and air. "Just tell me this, thief's kid to thief's kid: he did it, didn't he?"

"Don't be absurd," Kelly snarled, but the petite girl only moved closer.

"Oliver Kelly took that stone and built an empire from it."

"My grandfather was—"

"A visionary. A pioneer. The man who went into that chamber while the Miller family slept, and claimed the Cleopatra Emerald..." The girl pressed even closer, looked up into his eyes. "He was a thief, wasn't he?"

Kelly seemed trapped inside the small space, a thousand thoughts crashing inside his mind as he looked at the girl who was nothing, and hissed, "*Of course he was.*"

The lift rumbled to life. The doors opened.

"Katarina?" The expression on Maggie's face was part

panic, part relief. She looked at Kat as if wondering what, if any, strings were attached. "You're—"

"Here?" Kat finished for her. "Don't worry, Maggie." She turned and started for the doors. "There is no place that I would rather be."

As one of the world's best thieves, it was in Kat Bishop's blood – not just her nature – to stay away from spotlights. But there was something fitting, she thought, about being at Maggie's right hand while the woman moved down the centre aisle to take her place in the small section of empty seats at the front of the crowded room.

No, Kat realised a second later. Not empty. Not quite.

A single boy sat alone, a guard standing nearby.

"Madame, your orders…" the guard started, but Maggie silenced him with a wave and took her seat in the front row, leaving Kat to slide in beside Hale.

"Are you here to rescue me?" she asked.

"Maybe." He smiled.

She looked down at the plastic restraints that bound his wrists. "How's that going?"

He nodded slowly. "I'm working through a few things."

"Good." Kat nodded and turned her gaze to the front of the room. "So long as there's a plan."

"Oh –" he gave a slow, easy grin – "there is one."

Kat saw it all from her place at the front of the room – the way LaFont moved to the microphone, the nervous pacing of the auctioneer, who was standing by. The room was full of three hundred barely breathing people when the doors at the back squeaked open. Every head turned to see two more security guards appear, each holding a Bagshaw by the back of the neck (which might have been significantly less conspicuous had the Bagshaws not been dressed as chimney sweeps).

Kat turned back to Hale. "The Mary Poppins?"

"Seemed like a good idea at the time."

"Oh. Yeah. Obviously. Just so we're clear, this master plan of yours..."

"Might have a couple of kinks to work through," Hale admitted, then reached for her hand. As soon as he touched her, Kat knew there was no such thing as curses. People make and break their own fortunes – they are the masters of their own fate. And right then Kat wouldn't have changed a thing.

She kissed him, quick and feather soft.

"What was that for?" he asked.

Kat placed her fingers on his face and brought his forehead close to hers, touching as she whispered, "For luck."

LaFont was already at the podium by the time Kat turned around. "Ladies and gentlemen, *mesdames et messieurs.*" He took the room in slowly. It was the greatest moment in his life, Kat knew. The crowning glory. The find of a lifetime.

It brought her no small amount of sadness to have to ruin it.

Just then, the side doors swung open. Two more guards appeared, one holding a laptop, the other with a firm grip on a very blushing Simon.

Maggie turned to Kat, smiling, but at the front of the room, LaFont talked on.

"Before we begin, due to the magnitude of this offering, we have conceded to hold one final authentication – here, before these witnesses – to verify that this is the famed and once-lost Antony Emerald."

This was not news to any of the people in the room. In fact, the collectors and investors gathered were already quite familiar with the man from the Cairo Museum and the woman from India who was the most respected gemologist in the world. One by one, half a dozen experts were called and named, their credentials read, until the case with the green stone was finally opened.

Even though the stone had been officially authenticated before, the room still watched in rapt silence while the experts gathered around it for the purely ceremonial show.

But not Maggie; Maggie was looking directly at Kat.

"It's over, darling," she said, with a pat of Kat's hands. "I appreciate your enthusiasm." She let her gaze slide to Hale. "The dedication you children have shown. I do see a great deal of promise in you."

"Is that so?" Kat asked.

"Yes." Maggie laughed softly. Her eyes were almost kind. "It's almost like seeing myself."

"I'm not like you," Kat said again, the conversation in the car coming back to her, but Maggie was still unconvinced.

"Of course you are. Don't be ashamed that you've lost this

one," she said. "As I was telling your uncle before he left last night, he's done well with you. You are an excellent thief. But of course there are some holes in your education."

"Are there?" Hale asked.

Maggie ignored him.

"When this is over, you can come with me, Katarina. There's so much I can teach you."

"You sound confident, Maggie," Kat said.

There was no gloating in Maggie's smile when she said, "I am."

Another door swung open, and another guard appeared, this time with Gabrielle, who wore a black catsuit and rappelling harness.

That should have been the end, of course. Kat looked around the room at her beaten and battered crew, and it seemed the curse had won. In a few minutes, the bidding would begin, the cheque would be written, and the emerald would disappear into another country, behind another set of walls – perhaps not to be seen again for another thousand years.

It was almost over.

Kat felt Hale's hand in her own.

It was only just beginning.

"Ladies and gentlemen..." The gemologist from India had finally moved to the microphone. She gave an involuntary glance at the colleagues gathered behind her, then took a deep breath and finished, "it is the opinion of the experts assembled here that the gem known as the Antony Emerald is a magnificent specimen."

Maggie sighed, the softest sound – as if she had been holding her breath for fifty years and only then felt free to let it go.

The expert finished, "In fact, it is the most spectacular fake that any of us have ever seen."

FORTY-ONE

Chaos would not have been the word that Kat would have used. Chaos implies movement and action and fear. What followed was the quietest kind of panic that Kat had ever seen.

"There must be some... But it's been authenticated by... There must be some mistake!" LaFont cried, but the words were lost in the din of chatter that was growing inside the room, which, seconds before, had been as quiet and reverent as a church.

The crowd was talking. Heads were turning. But if anyone thought that Margaret Covington Godfrey Brooks had been part of the plot, all they needed to do was look at her to see that she was the most surprised of all.

In a moment, the shock seemed to fade, and Maggie was up and rushing to the emerald.

"Madame!" LaFont called. "Please, take your seat. Rest..."

But Maggie was not going to pass out. She wasn't at risk of suffering a stroke, and her heart, Kat knew, was far too fake to fail. The real threat, Kat knew, lay not in what might happen to Maggie, but in what Maggie might *do*.

"Madame, are you well?" LaFont had to know, but the woman merely pushed him aside as if he too were an elaborate fraud and had no worth whatsoever for her any more.

"But you're all here..." Maggie stopped and spun, her gaze passing from Gabrielle to Simon to the Bagshaws then back to Kat and Hale. "You're all here!"

"No, Maggie." Kat shook her head. "You missed one of us."

Through the chaos, it must have been easy not to notice that one final teen had appeared at the back of the room, surrounded by men in uniform and a woman who was very chic, incredibly beautiful, and completely immune to the madness.

Nick gave a small wave in Kat's direction, then turned to the woman by his side. His mother whispered something in his ear, then turned and called, "Mr Kelly!"

At first it seemed as if no one beyond Kat had heard her. The journalists were on their cell phones. Experts huddled close, trying to explain how the Antony had been so real just days before. Egos were bruised. Fortunes were dashed. The Cleopatra and her curse were the last things on anyone's mind until the woman with the British accent yelled, "Mr Oliver Kelly!"

"No comment," Kelly said, with a quick turn and dismissing wave.

"That's a shame." Amelia crossed one arm over the other. "I was hoping you might be able to explain this."

She pushed a button on a small device, and a moment later, a booming voice came through the speakers of the room. A grainy video began to play on the screens behind the podium.

"The Cleopatra Emerald is not cursed!"

"He took it, didn't he? What I can't decide is if he joined the Millers' expedition for the purpose of double-crossing them or if it was just dumb luck."

"My grandfather was not dumb."

"Of course he wasn't. If you ask me, he was a genius. That much treasure? It might have been the heist of the century."

"Oliver Kelly was no common criminal!"

"Who said anything about common? Just tell me this, thief's kid to thief's kid: he did it, didn't he?"

"Don't be absurd."

"Oliver Kelly took that stone and built an empire from it."

"My grandfather was—"

"A visionary. A pioneer. The man who went into that chamber while the Miller family slept, and claimed the Cleopatra Emerald. He was a thief, wasn't he?"

The angle of the camera was strange, as if someone had spent the morning riding around on the top of the lift, filming through the vents. It showed no more than black hair on a short girl, but there was no mistaking that Kelly was the man who stood shaking, loosening his tie as he admitted, *"Of course he was."*

A hushed silence washed over the room, and in that brief second even the Antony was forgotten.

"As I was saying, Mr Kelly, my name is Amelia Bennett, and I work for Interpol. If you don't mind, sir, we'd like to ask you a few questions."

Kat didn't stay to hear the stories and excuses, the denials and the lies. Hale had freed himself from his restraints, and as one arm fell gently around her shoulders, Kat felt the tension she'd been carrying there dissolve. At the back of the room, Hamish and Angus had slipped their guards as well. Simon too. Only Gabrielle remained.

Kat watched Nick walk to the guards that stood beside her cousin and tell them, "She's with us," and just that quickly they were free – all of them. No one stopped them at the doors. Outside the gates, not a single tourist seemed to care about the seven thieves who were walking away after stealing the most famous emerald in the world. Again.

For the first time since she'd arrived on the Riviera, Kat really saw the water. She really felt the sun. The Mediterranean was beautiful, she had to think, as they walked towards the cliffs.

"Katarina!" The voice called to her again, carried on the wind, and despite the sun and sea air, Kat's mind flashed back to New York. She could almost feel the freezing wind and rain, and she wondered what might have happened if she hadn't turned around. But then Kat stopped and shook her head. She looked at Hale, and that was when Kat Bishop finally managed to stop thinking.

"Katarina." Maggie was not running. The officers of Interpol had no interest in the woman who had been humiliated in such a public way. Her fifteen minutes in the spotlight were over, so the Antony would stay gone, buried, while the Cleopatra was left alone on centre stage.

And Maggie, Maggie was left to walk alone, out into the sun.

"How?" The word seemed to pain her, but there was no anger, no threat. Just professional curiosity as she stepped forward, defeat in her eyes. "You're a child, Katarina. A talented, intelligent girl, but...a child."

"I'm a thief, Maggie."

"Yes, of course. But...how?"

Kat felt her crew around her: Hamish's arm hung around Simon's shoulders; Gabrielle's delicate hands draped through the arms of Angus and Nick. Kat's own hand found Hale's, then, fingers interlacing, palms pressing together so tightly that Kat knew nothing could come between them. Nothing. She looked at him. No one.

"It's easy," Kat said, "when you don't have to do it alone."

"But your uncle—"

"Played his part to perfection, don't you think?" Gabrielle said. "I guess maybe he hasn't forgiven you after all." Kat watched the shock seep into Maggie's eyes while her cousin talked. "I mean, without him, you probably never would have brought the Cleopatra to town, and without that...well..."

Kat pushed her hair out of her eyes and studied the woman

who might have been her future. Maybe. But then Kat felt Hale squeeze her hand, root her, ground her to that time and place, and Kat knew that as long as she never let go, then she and Maggie would never share the same footsteps.

"But..." Maggie started, stumbling for words.

"You still don't get it, do you, Margaret?" Kat smiled almost sadly. "We never had to steal the Antony. All we had to do was get it next to the Cleopatra and switch the signs."

2 WEEKS
AFTER THE AUCTION

URUGUAY
or maybe it was
PARAGUAY...

FORTY-TWO

Though the story of the emerald called the Antony had run in all the papers, it was not the sort of news that mattered long in a place like Valle Dorado. The summer had been too hot, the rainy season too long, and there was too much work to do to worry about a green stone that was two thousand years old and half a world away.

Or so the people said. But the whispers, Kat had noticed, the whispers were always the last to die.

Sitting between Hale and Gabrielle at a café on the sunny side of the square, Kat tried not to think about the papers that lay untouched on the ground at Hale's feet. She knew too well what they would say...

That the Antony was a hoax. A beautiful fake. A delicate con. That many of the experts who had initially sworn the emerald was authentic were now attributing their mistake to faulty instruments and jet lag.

If anyone went looking for the woman known as Margaret Covington Godfrey Brooks, they did not find her. She was gone almost as quickly as the Antony, dissolved into the tourists and the crowds, washed away like the surf and the sand, but Kat knew she was still out there. Kat knew someday she, like the Antony, might be seen again.

Across the square, there was a fountain with a statue of Saint Christopher, a church opening its doors after morning Mass. She saw school children and merchants, heard the bells chiming, telling the world that it was time to get on with life.

"How long?" Hale asked.

"Three minutes," both girls said at the same time.

The people on the square that day had noticed the three young people who sat at a table, ordering lemonade. The girls wore white dresses, and the boy a straw hat, and they looked almost like a painting, sitting there, soaking up the sun.

When the drinks came, Gabrielle crossed one long leg over the other, and Kat had to ask, "How's the ankle?"

Gabrielle smiled. "Good as new."

Maybe the curse was broken and over, or maybe it had never been real at all. All Kat knew for certain was that there are some things even the best artists can't fake. There are some events that even the best thieves can never plan. And real love ...real love can never be split in two.

She wondered for a second about the Antony, and something told her that the stories were true – that it was out there somewhere, lost and waiting – but Kat also knew she wouldn't look for it.

What Kat really needed, she had already found.

"To Uncle Eddie," Hale said, raising his glass. "The ultimate inside man."

Gabrielle repeated the toast, but Kat couldn't bring herself to say the words.

"What?" Gabrielle asked.

"Do you think he still loves her?" She kept her eyes trained on the other side of the street as a well-dressed man walked into a bank, seemingly oblivious to the dump truck that sat idling a mere twenty feet away.

Kat looked down at her lemonade. "Do you think he betrayed the love of his life...because of us?"

"She used the name Romani, Kat," was Gabrielle's answer. "And besides..." She let the words draw out. Her gaze went to the distance, and there was a sense of peace in the way she said, "*We're* the love of his life." She raised her glass again. "To family."

This time Kat couldn't help but join in.

"So isn't it time for the..." Hale started, but trailed off when, half a block away, a loud explosion sounded and a spiral of black smoke billowed up, temporarily blocking out the sky.

"Yep," Kat said.

"And your dad's sure the organised crime ring that's sitting on this stash doesn't know its real value?" Hale asked, concerned.

"Well, we're about to find out," Kat said as a man ran to the fountain, then called in rapid Spanish that he needed all available hands at the back of the church. "Wow. Uncle Felix's leg is doing a lot better."

"Yeah." Gabrielle gave an enthusiastic nod. "He's getting

around really well."

There was chaos on the square as people yelled and smoke rose, but the three teens sat quietly, waiting, as Uncle Eddie climbed into the truck and drove away.

"So," Hale said, watching the smoke rise and the Bagshaws run. "Where to now?"

Kat stood and downed her drink in one swallow, set the glass back on the table, and turned into the sun.

"Well, see, there's this cave in Switzerland I really need to find." She slipped on her sunglasses; was already in the middle of the street when she turned and looked back at Hale and Gabrielle. "You coming?"

Don't miss the next thrilling

HEIST SOCIETY

adventure, *Perfect Scoundrels.*

ACKNOWLEDGEMENTS

If there's one thing that writing the *Heist Society* books has taught me, it's that you are is only as good as your crew.

I could never have finished this book without the tremendous support and keen editorial eyes of Catherine Onder. I owe so much to Stephanie Lurie, Deborah Bass, Dina Sherman and the rest of the Disney-Hyperion family, who are always willing to shelter me when I'm on the run and get me whatever gear I need.

I'm deeply indebted to Jenny Meyer, Whitney Lee, Sarah Self and especially Kristin Nelson and everyone at the Nelson Literary Agency for their constant loyalty and unwavering dedication. They are the best fences in the business.

Words cannot express my gratitude to Heidi Leinbach for all she does to make these books possible and keep me sane. Plus, she's always there to drive the getaway car.

My crew would not be complete without Jen Barnes, Holly Black, Rose Brock, Maureen Johnson, Carrie Ryan and Bob, who are always willing to blow things up, dangle off rooftops, and do whatever it takes to help me survive the long con that is this business.

And, of course, I owe it all to my father, mother and big sister, who have taught me everything I know.

BKMRK

Find your place

Want to be the first to hear
about the best new teen and YA reads?

Want exclusive content, offers
and competitions?

Want to chat about books with people
who love them as much as you do?

Look no further . . .

bkmrk.co.uk

 @TeamBkmrk   /TeamBkmrk

 @TeamBkmrk   TeamBkmrk

See you there!